"What are you doing here?" Smith asked.

Julie Ann said, "I called the sheriff and got you some backup."

"I told you to stay in your beauty shop."

"Did you catch the shooter?"

"No, there were a couple of shell casings on the roof but that's all."

"See? It was safe to come out."

The absurdity of her statement made him want to shake some sense into her. Clenching his fists instead, Smith said, "You know better than that."

"This isn't a combat zone," Julie Ann argued. "Lighten up."

In a way she was right. But he couldn't expect a civilian to understand what it was like to come under fire.

He reached out and gently cupped her shoulder. "Come on, I'll walk you back to your shop and we can tell the sheriff what we saw."

Smith pulled her closer. When he'd promised Julie Ann's brother he'd look after her, Smith hadn't dreamed things would take such an ominous turn.

Books by Valerie Hansen

Love Inspired Suspense

*Her Brother's Keeper
The Danger Within
*Out of the Depths
Deadly Payoff
*Shadow of Turning
Hidden in the Wall
*Nowhere to Run
*No Alibi

*Serenity, Arkansas

Love Inspired

*The Wedding Arbor
*The Troublesome Angel
*The Perfect Couple
*Second Chances
*Love One Another
*Blessings of the Heart
*Samantha's Gift
*Everlasting Love
The Hamilton Heir
*A Treasure of the Heart

Love Inspired Historical

Frontier Courtship
Wilderness Courtship

VALERIE HANSEN

was thirty when she awoke to the presence of the Lord in her life and turned to Jesus. In the years that followed she worked with young children, both in church and secular environments. She also raised a family of her own and played foster mother to a wide assortment of furred and feathered critters.

Married to her high school sweetheart since age seventeen, she now lives in an old farmhouse she and her husband renovated with their own hands. She loves to hike the wooded hills behind the house and reflect on the marvelous turn her life has taken. Not only is she privileged to reside among the loving, accepting folks in the breathtakingly beautiful Ozark mountains of Arkansas, she also gets to share her personal faith by telling the stories of her heart for Steeple Hill Books.

Life doesn't get much better than that!

NO ALIBI

VALERIE HANSEN

Steeple
Hill®

Published by Steeple Hill Books™

STEEPLE HILL BOOKS

Steeple
Hill®

Recycling programs
for this product may
not exist in your area.

ISBN-13: 978-0-373-44341-3

NO ALIBI

This edition published by arrangement with Steeple Hill Books.

® and TM are trademarks of Steeple Hill Books, used under license. Trademarks indicated with ® are registered in the United States Patent and Trademark Office, the Canadian Trade Marks Office and in other countries.

www.SteepleHill.com

Printed in U.S.A.

When I am afraid, I will trust in you. In God, whose
word I praise, in God I trust; I will not be afraid.
—*Psalms* 56:3–4

Given my love and appreciation for the wonderful people in my life, I hardly know where to begin. I am so blessed it's scary!

As always, a special hug for my husband. Not only is he a great guy, he can cook! And he does, especially when I'm busy writing more books. Hey, maybe *that's* why I've tried to stay so busy.

PROLOGUE

Under the cover of a nearly moonless night, the well-dressed man ordered the driver of his limousine to park behind a bank of metal storage buildings where they couldn't be seen from the street.

When his local accomplice climbed in to join him as planned, the executive edged closer to the opposite door and tried to mask his disdain. "Are you sure this will work the way I explained? I don't want any slipups." Arching an eyebrow, he waited for his rough-hewn, young confederate to answer.

"It'll work. Ol' Lester'll never know what hit him. And he knows better than to open his yap and rat us out."

"Us?" The silk-suited, older man straightened his tie and smiled malevolently. "There is no *us*, Denny. You and I have never met, remember?"

"Yeah, yeah. I remember. Just see to it that I get my fair share and we'll have no problems, Mr. Evans."

"No names!" The command **was** unmistakably a threat. He'd meant it to be. Not only **did** his own future depend upon the success of this plan, he had others to answer to. Others who would be even less forgiving than he was.

"Okay. Don't go gettin' all het up. When are you gonna sic the cops on him?"

"Just as soon as you let me know he's shipped out a couple of batches of booze. We don't want to shut him down too early. He has to look as guilty as sin."

"I still don't get it," the younger, jeans-clad man said. "Why set him up to make good moonshine and then take him down?"

"You don't have to understand any more than I choose to tell you." His eyes narrowed and his jaw clenched. "I'll take care of the details. You just do your job. And keep me advised."

"Yes, sir." Denny gave a halfhearted salute and reached for the door handle. "Another week or two ought to do it. I got him plenty of sugar and yeast. He's picking up the sacks of corn from the feed mill, like you said he should."

"All right. Meet me back here in one week, same day, same time, and I'll decide what happens next."

"Lester ain't gonna like it when he's arrested. How you gonna keep him from figurin' out I'm the one that turned him in?"

"I said I'd take care of it and I will," Evans assured him. "Now get going."

"Yes, sir."

As the limousine slipped away into the moonless night and headed for the highway, Evans opened his cell phone, pushed Redial and quickly made a connection.

"It's all set," he said.

He listened a moment, then replied, "Don't worry about Denny. He doesn't have a clue as to what's really going on and he won't say a word about the old man being framed, either."

He chuckled at the query on the other end of the line, then answered, "No, he won't get wise or change his mind and sell out to the Feds. He won't have time to. I have a strong feeling poor Denny is going to meet with a tragic accident long before this bootlegging case goes to trial."

ONE

Julie Ann Jones loved her career. There was something very rewarding about running the Serenity Salon. She'd always been artistic and she knew cosmetology was the perfect way to put her God-given talent to good use. Her friends had been delighted by her success, which helped make up for the fact that she hadn't gotten even the slightest inkling of support from her parents.

She usually kept her own honey-brown hair short but had decided to let it grow in order to donate it to an organization that provided wigs for juvenile cancer patients. The longer length was driving her crazy but she was determined to hold out for the sake of the charity.

Her only employee, Sherilyn Fox, was another of her community projects. A high school dropout, Sherilyn had desperately needed a job, so as soon as she'd graduated from beauty school, Julie Ann had hired her. Seeing the girl's pride and self-worth increasing daily had made Julie Ann feel as if she were looking into a mirror and watching the birth of her own hard-won independence.

Sherilyn burst through the door of the otherwise

quiet beauty shop and waved a handful of mail. "You aren't going to like this, boss."

"Why? More bills? What a surprise."

"Uh-uh." She shook her blond, spiked hair and made a silly face. "Worse."

"Nothing could be worse than bills," Julie Ann said. "Trust me. I know." She grimaced, thinking of the sacrifices she'd made in order to avoid having to ask her parents—or anyone else—for financial help. She was determined to succeed on her own, and so far, so good, despite her father's criticism.

"Then I guess you've never gotten a jury summons before, huh?"

"A what?" Julie Ann snatched the envelope from Sherilyn's hand, tore it open and unfolded the contents. Her hazel eyes widened and her shoulders sagged. "I don't believe this. How can I take time off to serve on a jury? I have a business to run."

"Hey, it's not like the courthouse is that far away." Sherilyn pointed out the beauty shop window that fronted the Serenity square. "You could hit it with a rock from here."

"I'd like to do that right about now," Julie Ann admitted, "but they'd probably arrest me." She stared at the summons in her hand. "I can't spare the time away. Do you suppose they'd excuse me if I explained my problem?"

"Maybe. I suppose it's worth a try."

"I'm sure it is." Refolding the summons, she stuffed it into the pocket of her pastel flowered smock and started for the door. "I don't have another appointment until Louella's perm. Hold down the fort for me, will you?"

"Sure. You going to beg?"

"If I have to," Julie Ann said with a quirky half-smile. "I am friends with a lot of folks over at the courthouse. Surely somebody will be able to help me get excused."

"Are you positive that's the right thing to do?" Sherilyn asked. "What if all Christians begged off? Who'd be left?"

Julie Ann was still mulling over that question when she stepped out of her shop and scanned the broad, tree-lined street that flanked the town square. In a way, the girl was right. Who would be left? Then again, the Bible also cautioned believers to be good stewards of what God had given them. If she neglected her business, wouldn't that be a sin, too?

Satisfied with that, Julie Ann hurried across the street. She could not serve on a jury. Not if she wanted to keep her business afloat, let alone flourishing. A spiky-haired assistant like Sherilyn was fine for the younger crowd but older women weren't likely to trust her to touch their hair. Julie Ann understood that. Not that she was that much older at twenty-five. She was simply more traditional.

She glanced at her watch as she started up the court-house walkway. Hopefully she had enough spare time to see the powers that be and get this mess straightened out.

Reaching for the handle of the heavy glass door, she was almost run over by a familiar, broad-shouldered man who was exiting.

His gruff "Excuse me" was not accompanied by a smile. On the contrary, he was glaring at her through coffee-dark eyes. Smith Burnett's face looked so different from the way she usually saw it that she was taken aback.

"Smith? What's wrong?"

He paused long enough to hold the door for her. "This," he said, waving a crumpled piece of paper.

Julie Ann immediately recognized the form. "Jury duty?"

"Yes. They said only the judge himself can excuse me. How am I supposed to run a real estate business if I'm cooling my heels in a jury box?"

She nodded as she fished her own summons out of the pocket of her smock. "I know exactly how you feel. I was hoping…"

"Well, don't hold your breath," he said, glancing down the empty hallway of the old, brick building. "I got nowhere. They just told me to fill out a questionnaire and leave the rest to the judge's discretion."

"In that case, if you want a haircut from me you'd best be getting it soon," Julie Ann said, assessing his thick, dark hair. She didn't want to remember how it had felt to run her fingertips over it when she'd been much younger and *far* too impressionable. "I'm afraid I may be tied up soon."

"Yeah. Me too."

Turning away from him and starting down the hallway, she was suddenly aware that her heart was beating fast. It was obviously because she was upset about the summons, discounting the disturbing realization that her shakiness began when she'd encountered Smith. She'd never seen him that animated, that forceful, that… The only other word that came to mind was *masculine*.

After his stint as a Marine and subsequent return to

Serenity, he'd seemed different, yes, but not *this* different. This was a darker, more dynamic aspect of his personality than she'd ever imagined, let alone glimpsed, and it had affected her all the way from the roots of her hair to her toes.

When she left the courthouse later, Smith was waiting for her. He could tell by her crestfallen expression that she, too, had been denied a reprieve.

All he said was "Hi."

"Hi. I thought you were headed back to work."

"I was. I decided to wait and see if you had any more success than I did."

"Nope. They told me a computer makes the selections and everyone has to take a turn. Now, it's mine. And yours."

He nodded. "I apologize for snapping at you earlier. You caught me at a bad time."

"No problem."

Hoping she truly did forgive him, he watched her expression closely as he asked, "So, do you have time to cut my hair now?"

"Not really. How about first thing tomorrow?"

"Sounds good."

"We won't all be picked to serve, you know," Julie Ann said, shading her eyes from the sun to look up at him. "The county clerk assured me that most cases are settled by a plea bargain."

"I know. But since we both have very good reasons for not wanting to be chosen, what do you want to bet we are?"

"I never bet," she said with a soft laugh, "but I know exactly what you mean. Maybe I should plan on bringing my scissors to the jury waiting room and working there. I could use the extra business."

He was surprised by her upbeat attitude in the face of such trying circumstances. She had not always been that easygoing. Far from it. Perhaps maturity had mellowed her even more than he'd realized. The stubborn, rebellious teen he recalled from years ago would have pitched a royal fit.

"Well, as long as you're not mad, I'm satisfied," Smith said. "Wouldn't want a woman who stands behind me wielding sharp scissors to be holding a grudge."

"Smart man."

Julie Ann really had become more appealing, Smith mused, especially since she'd let her hair grow. Although she now kept that dark-honey-colored hair pulled back, there were always a few silky tendrils that escaped, falling across her cheeks and making her look even more attractive. The funny thing was, every time he saw her, his personal interest increased.

Now that Smith had reached his early thirties, the difference in their ages had become less important than it had seemed seven or eight years ago when he'd escorted her to her senior prom. That one evening had caused him nothing but grief. If he hadn't been deployed overseas shortly thereafter, there would have been no painless way to avoid Julie Ann. The dozens of mushy letters she'd written to him had been bad enough. Nothing had discouraged her. Not even his attempts to let her down easy.

But things were very different now, weren't they?

His current dilemma was deciding whether or not to deepen the casual friendship they had finally developed and see if they might actually be right for each other.

The last thing Smith wanted to do was explain to her brother, Ben, why she had developed another ridiculous crush on him. The first time had been bad enough. And since he'd promised he'd look after her while Ben and his unit remained abroad, Smith had no intention of going back on his word, even if that meant he had to protect her from *himself*.

"See you tomorrow morning then," she said, backing away. "Gotta run."

Pensive, Smith watched her safely cross the street and enter her shop before he turned to scan the rest of the square. The recently reelected sheriff, Harlan Allgood, was helping a handcuffed, shackled man clad in a bright orange jumpsuit out of a patrol car. Harlan was a good man, if a bit naive. Chances were, the skinny kid he had arrested was not nearly as nefarious as those cuffs and leg irons made him appear.

Dismissing the sight, Smith thought about Julie Ann again and smiled. He'd get his hair cut first thing tomorrow morning, mostly as an excuse to see her.

His smile grew into a lopsided grin. Everything would be fine as long as she didn't notice that he really wasn't in need of a trim.

"They've arrested Lester's stupid nephew and they're lookin' for Lester," Denny dutifully reported, climbing into the familiar limo for the third Thursday night in a row.

"I know."

"Got 'em for making moonshine, just like we planned."

"I know that, too."

"Word is, the Feds want Lester real bad and as soon as they catch him, he's gonna be sent off to Little Rock for trial."

"I think not," his well-dressed companion said. "I'm arranging to have him tried right here, first, for something else. The federal government can have whatever's left of him when we're done."

"No matter. It shouldn't take long. I mean, what else can he be guilty of that matters around here?"

"A crime that will definitely take precedence over running an illegal still."

"Like what?"

"Like murder," Evans said quietly, menacingly.

"Lester? He's quiet as a mouse. He'd never kill nobody."

"I didn't say he did it, you fool. I said he was going to be *tried* for it."

"But who's dead?"

The smooth-talking businessman merely smiled. "That's none of your concern, Denny. You've done your job and it's over." He reached a gloved hand into his suit coat's inside pocket and withdrew a bulging envelope. "Here's your fee. Now get out and get lost."

"Yes, sir." The younger man did as he was instructed, slammed the car door, then leaned down to cup his hands around his mouth and shout through the closed window. "You never did tell me. Who's Lester gonna be blamed for killin'?"

On a simple hand signal from his boss, the limo

driver dropped the car into gear and drove away from the scene.

Evans was laughing to himself as he settled against the plush leather of the car's rear seat and murmured softly, "You."

TWO

By the time Smith arrived at her shop the next morning, Julie Ann was already upset by the rumors she'd heard. Forcing a smile, she shook out a plastic cape as she said, "Good morning."

"Morning." He plopped into her chair and sighed while she wrapped the cape around his neck and prepared him for his haircut. His gaze was somber when it met hers in the mirror. "I take it you've heard."

"About Denny Hanford? Yes. It's all over town. It's hard to believe he was actually murdered."

Smith was nodding. "I didn't believe it either, at first. They found him last night, by the storage yard out on Highway 9."

"Poor Denny. Who would do such a thing?"

"Lester Taney was seen in the area. Denny apparently tipped the law to the location of Lester's bootlegging operation and Lester shot him for it."

"That's unbelievable." Her lips pressed into a thin line as she recalled her high school years. "Denny never was the sharpest pencil in the box but he always seemed to have a pretty good heart."

"Not according to some of the good old boys around here. You should hear all the talk over at the café."

"It still doesn't make sense to me. Bootlegging went out of style with the end of Prohibition."

"Apparently not. We live in a dry county, and with taxes on liquor so high, I guess it's still profitable."

Julie Ann picked up her scissors and began combing and snipping Smith's thick, dark hair. "You don't think we'll be called for that jury, do you?"

"I doubt it. With the way everybody in town knows everybody else, I can't see how they'd expect to find an impartial jury around here."

Her eyebrows arched as her gaze again met his in the mirror. "That's true."

Eventually laying aside her comb and scissors, she reached for the clippers. This part could be a bit tricky but she was so used to doing it, it was practically automatic.

Consequently, when Smith cleared his throat and asked, "Didn't you and Denny date years ago?" her clippers jerked and strayed into the back of his hair above the area she'd intended to trim.

Julie Ann's heartfelt "Ack!" made Smith jump and sent her errant cut even higher.

She stepped back, appalled. "I'm so sorry!"

"How bad is it?"

"Not that bad. I can even it up."

"Before you take my ear off, maybe you should answer my question. Did you date Denny Hanford?"

"No. Yes. Sort of. We had mutual friends and we all used to run around together." Although her first instinct had been to deny any connection, she certainly wasn't going to lie. After all, there was no real tie between her and the poor, dead young man.

She met Smith's steady gaze in the mirror again. "He'd failed a couple of grades and wound up in my graduating class. There weren't very many of us so we all knew each other, okay?"

As she bent lower to reshape the thick hair on the back of Smith's head, she had to force herself to concentrate on what she was doing. Were others going to ask her about her relationship with Denny? Did it really matter? She supposed not. He had been a much closer friend to her older brother, Ben, and when Ben, like Smith, had joined the Marines, she'd been glad to see him far removed from Denny's questionable influence.

Would that be enough to disqualify her from serving on the murder trial's jury? Perhaps. And perhaps not. Either way, it wasn't up to her. If the Good Lord wanted her to serve, she'd have to. That was all there was to it.

The notion of holding another person's life in her hands, however, made her feel queasy.

Smith looked over his shoulder at her. "You okay?"

"Sure. Fine. Just overworked. Sherilyn didn't show up this morning and when I phoned to ask her why, she couldn't stop crying long enough to tell me."

"Uh-oh. Were she and Denny involved?"

"I don't think so. She tells me a lot about her love life—usually more than I'd like to hear—and she's never mentioned his name."

"Still, they probably ran around with some of the same people."

Julie Ann reluctantly agreed. "You're right. Sherilyn had a pretty hard life until recently so that theory fits. I haven't had much success getting her interested in the youth activities at my church but I keep trying."

"She just needs to grow up more before she develops common sense."

Julie Ann met his glance in the mirror, then averted her eyes. "Like I did, you mean?"

"I never said that."

"No, but you were thinking it."

When Smith didn't contradict her, she felt her cheeks warming with embarrassment. They had never talked about her actions following their one date but she knew he hadn't been infatuated with her, as she'd hoped back then.

She huffed and pressed her lips into a thin line. That was the understatement of the century. If he hadn't come to her for haircuts after his military buzz cut had grown out, she'd have assumed he never forgave her for the way she'd pursued him. She certainly wouldn't have blamed him for avoiding her completely. If their roles had been reversed, that's probably what she would have done. She was a lot smarter these days—even where Smith was concerned.

As Smith had feared, he and Julie Ann were both notified to report for jury selection a few weeks later. He followed her and several others into the courtroom. It wasn't like the depictions he'd seen on TV and in the movies. There were fifteen rows of padded, armless chairs facing a small, raised, oak-paneled area beneath the Arkansas seal, which was flanked by national and state flags.

Tables were arranged on either side of the judge's bench and attorneys were already poring over the questionnaires he and the others had filled out.

Smith would have taken a seat beside Julie Ann if other women had not immediately crowded around her and begun chattering like a gaggle of excited geese.

Julie Ann's name was the fifth one called. She was graceful and pretty as ever, he noted, although she looked terribly tense as she faced the attorneys, Grimes and Lazarus.

"Your name, please?" the portly Grimes asked.

"Julie Ann Jones."

"And your residence is in Fulton County, Ms. Jones?"

"Yes. I live in Heart, off Squirrel Hill Road."

"How long have you lived there?"

"Six years. The house was my grandfather's."

Smith could tell she was terribly nervous because not only was her voice shaky, she was clasping her hands together so tightly that her fingers were white against the pale blue of her dress. He didn't doubt that she was taking this a lot more seriously than most of her peers and he feared her attitude would make her a good choice as a juror.

"Were you acquainted with the victim, Denny Hanford, Ms. Jones?"

"Sure. We were kids together and we went to the same schools. Everybody in Serenity did."

He gestured toward the defendant's table where an

old man in an orange jumpsuit sat, his eyes downcast and shoulders slumped. "How about the accused, Lester Taney?"

"I've seen him around."

As soon as Grimes said, "The people approve," the judge addressed the defense attorney. "Mr. Lazarus? Do you have any questions for Ms. Jones?"

He shook his graying head, remembering Evans's instructions. His Adam's apple bobbed in his gangly neck. "None, your honor."

"Then we have our first juror." The judge gestured at the jury box. "Please have a seat, Ms. Jones."

As Julie Ann took her place, her hazel gaze found Smith's in the crowd and lingered. She reminded him of a frightened doe, frozen in the middle of the road by the headlights of an oncoming car and unable to jump out of the way of obvious danger.

And she wasn't the only one who was on edge. Smith didn't know why, but his senses were as heightened as if he were back in a combat zone and expecting incoming enemy fire at any second.

Three more jurors were seated before the group broke for lunch. Smith's name had not been called so he was confident it wouldn't be against the rules to speak to Julie Ann. Falling into step beside her, he left the courthouse with the rest of the group.

Julie Ann stretched and rubbed her neck. "I'm one big knot of tension already. I can't imagine what the real trial will do to my nerves."

"I'm sorry," he said, truly commiserating. "Some of

us are going to go grab a bite to eat at Hickory Station. Want to join us?"

"As soon as I check with Sherilyn and see how the shop is running without me," Julie Ann said. "I canceled all my regulars but there are usually several walk-ins in the mornings."

"I take it she's doing better?"

"Yes. The funny thing is, she's never told me why she was so upset. I expected her to explain when she showed up for work again but she's acting as if nothing happened."

"That's better than leaving you in the lurch when you need to keep the shop open while you're gone."

"Boy, that's the truth."

He matched Julie Ann's brisk pace as she crossed the courthouse lawn and then the street. They were almost to the beauty shop when Smith heard a faint crack of sound that made him jump. His military training kicked in with such force that he almost threw himself to the ground and took her with him.

Sheltering Julie Ann with his body, he shoved her through the doorway instead.

"What are you…?"

He wasn't deterred. Nor did he quit pushing her until they were both well inside. Quickly assessing the room, he spotted the evidence of what he'd feared.

"Look. Up there," Smith said, pointing to the shop's front window.

Julie Ann gasped. "Oh my…."

"Somebody just took a shot at us."

"No way." As she started toward the front of the

salon she kept peering at the tiny, round hole in the window.

Sherilyn joined her. "Whoa. Bummer. I told you those kids with BB guns were going to hit us eventually."

Incredulous, Smith placed himself between the women and the window, facing them, his arms outstretched to form a barrier. "Stay away from the glass. I'm telling you, that's no BB."

"Nonsense," Julie Ann argued. "It's just a little bitty hole. What else could it be?"

"Small caliber. Maybe a .22," Smith said, glancing over his shoulder. "And from the looks of the pattern, it had to have come from high up. Maybe the courthouse."

"Now you're being ridiculous. This is Serenity. It's the middle of the day. Nobody would be shooting around here, let alone aiming at us."

Smith was about to contradict her when a second bullet hit the window behind him. He'd heard that sound often enough to react without hesitation.

Launching himself at the women, he dove for the floor with an arm around each of them. Rolling as he hit, he cradled their fall with his shoulders and the momentum carried them all out of the path of the firing.

One more half-turn and he had them almost beneath the counter at Julie Ann's station. He shoved them fully under her station, then leaped to his feet. "Stay put. Don't move a muscle. Do you hear me?"

Not waiting for their answers, he bolted for the door, straight-armed it, and raced across the street toward the area where he was positive the shots had originated.

* * *

Julie Ann was breathless. Speechless. What had just happened? Could Smith have been right? It seemed impossible, yet he was the one with combat training and he did act totally convinced.

She peeked out far enough to look at her front window. There were two distinct holes in it now, separated by several feet. She gasped and ducked back under the counter.

Lying beside her, her employee was sobbing hysterically into cupped hands.

"It's okay, Sherilyn. We're fine," she said before realizing that the girl might have been injured. "Are you okay? Did it hurt you?"

"N-no." She stifled a sob. "What happened?"

"I don't know. But at least nobody was hit." It suddenly occurred to her that Smith's back had been to the glass when it was hit the second time. She'd assumed that his actions had merely been tactical. Perhaps he had been shot! If he'd been hurt because she had failed to follow his instructions to stay away from the window, she'd never forgive herself.

Julie Ann patted the weeping girl on the shoulder as she raised up and edged partway out from under the counter. "You'll be safe if you stay here."

"No! Don't leave me!"

"I'm not going far," Julie Ann said, beginning to crawl away. "I'm just going to grab a phone to call the sheriff."

"He must have heard the shots."

"Not unless he was close by. I was right here and I didn't realize what was happening." But thank the Lord

Smith did, she added silently. If he hadn't been with them, hadn't reacted so quickly and gotten them out of the line of fire, no telling what shape they'd be in right now. That thought tied her stomach in a knot.

She raised up just enough to reach the portable phone, grabbed it and slid back under the overhanging shelf where she displayed the shampoos and conditioners she offered for sale. Hands shaking, she punched in 9-1-1.

It seemed to take forever for the dispatcher to answer.

When someone finally said, "Nine-one-one operator. Please state your emergency," Julie Ann was trembling so badly she could hardly get the words out.

"This—this is the Serenity Salon. We've been shot at," she stammered. "Right here on Main Street. It came from the courthouse."

"Ma'am? Are you injured?"

"No. No, we're fine. Smith Burnett went across the street after them. Please hurry!"

"Stay right where you are and don't hang up," the dispatcher said. "We're sending a unit."

Sherilyn grabbed her arm. "What did they say?"

"To stay here and wait on the line." Julie Ann thrust the phone at the girl. "Here. You do it."

"Why? Where are you going?"

"After Smith," Julie Ann said, starting to crawl away. "I'll sneak out the back door and circle around."

"No! Don't go. I can't stay here by myself. I can't!"

"You'll be fine. The sheriff's office is on the phone and someone will be here in a few minutes," she called over her shoulder.

"You're *crazy!*" The younger woman was shouting,

sobbing and screaming hysterically. "We're all going to get killed—just like Denny!"

There was no way Julie Ann could force herself to sit there and twiddle her thumbs when Smith might be in worse danger. Or wounded. Or both. He could very well have been on the receiving end of that last bullet and had managed to give chase in spite of it.

That thought cut her to the quick. She hesitated only long enough to peer out the rear door, then threw it open and darted into the alleyway.

Staying close to the brick wall, she crept far enough to spy the courthouse before hesitating. A black-and-white cop car was pulling up to the front of her shop while another slid to a stop across the street. That was good enough for her.

Running, she made it across Main and reached the courthouse door mere seconds after the sheriff. His gun wasn't drawn but he did have his palm resting on the holster.

"Smith Burnett's in there, Harlan. Don't shoot him," she warned hoarsely.

He stopped, stiffened. "Get back."

"No way."

Although he didn't turn, he was clearly aware of who she was because he countered with, "This is a job for me and my deputy, Miz Julie. If you get in the way I'll arrest you. I mean it."

She gritted her teeth. "It was my shop somebody was shooting at."

"All the more reason to stay clear," Harlan said. "I won't fire unless somebody points a gun at me. I promise."

What could she do? She'd known Harlan all her life and doubted that he'd actually arrest her if she defied him, yet anything was possible in a crisis situation. Which this clearly was, she added, chagrined.

The urge to know for sure that Smith was all right was so strong she almost entered anyway. Only the fact that he suddenly appeared at the base of the stairs leading to the upper floors stopped her.

Seeing him alive and well brought tears to Julie Ann's eyes. She blinked them away rather than let on how moved she was. She'd made the mistake of throwing herself at the poor man once and it had taken her years to live that down. She still cherished the photo of them that had been taken at her senior prom though she rarely looked at it. Her days of mooning over the image of the handsome Marine standing beside her in his dark blue dress uniform were over.

She sobered, remembering the moment when her brother had confessed his part in arranging her prom date. Smith had been doing a favor for Ben, not escorting her because he cared for her. And, because Smith had been so polite, so gentlemanly, she had reacted as if the good-looking Marine had suddenly fallen madly in love with her.

Now, there he stood, out of breath and speaking privately with the sheriff. If he had even noticed that she was present, he hadn't let on. Well, fine. Now that she knew Smith was all right, she'd go back to her shop and pretend she'd never left it.

Turning, she saw the idling patrol car and shivered. Since she was now thinking more clearly than she had been scant minutes ago, she realized that stepping into the street might very well make her a target. Preserving her pride was not worth that risk. She'd stay. And take the consequences. Even if Harlan didn't arrest her she knew she was in for a talking-to because there was no way Smith would let her actions slide. Not after he'd given her specific instructions to stay put.

When she looked back and saw the fire in his eyes, she knew her assumption had been correct.

He started toward her.

Julie Ann stood her ground, chin up, spine stiff. If he asked her why she was there, she was going to tell him the truth. Well, most of it, anyway. The embarrassing details regarding her personal concern for him she'd keep to herself.

Smith was so angry, so frustrated, he almost didn't trust himself to speak. "What are *you* doing here?"

"I called the sheriff and got you some help."

"I told you to stay in your shop."

"Did you catch the shooter?"

"No. There were a couple of shell casings on the roof but that's all."

"See? It was safe to come out."

The absurdity of her statement hit him in the gut and made him want to shake some sense into her. Clenching his fists instead, he said, "You know better than that."

"This isn't the inner city and it isn't a combat zone, either," Julie Ann argued. "Lighten up, Smith."

He took a deep breath to help him regain his composure. In a way, she was right. He couldn't expect a civilian to understand what it felt like to come under fire; to wonder if the next second was going to bring instant death or if your buddies were going to be blown to bits right before your eyes.

Demonstrating a calmness he didn't feel, he reached out and gently cupped her shoulder, turning and guiding her as he did so. "Come on. I'll walk you back to your shop and we can tell the deputy what we saw while Harlan checks out the courthouse."

"I wonder why somebody is mad at me?"

Smith pulled her closer, determined to keep himself between her and any perceived threat. When he'd promised Ben that he'd look after his little sister for him, Smith hadn't dreamed things would take such an ominous turn.

Alert and scanning everything along the street as they crossed, Smith echoed her question. Who could be doing this to Julie Ann? And why? She didn't seem to have an enemy in the world, let alone one who would shoot at her.

Praise God they had lousy aim, Smith added, wondering if the assailant had actually meant to miss. He sure hoped so, because he couldn't stick with Julie Ann 24/7 and if that person wasn't caught, there was a good chance something like this would happen again. Maybe with worse results.

THREE

"I think you should tell the judge what happened," Smith said on their way back to the courthouse after a grilling by Harlan and his deputy, Boyd.

Julie Ann rolled her eyes. "And accomplish what? Make him think I had somebody shoot my window just so I could be excused? If I hadn't had to send Sherilyn home to calm down, the shop would still be open."

"Well, you can't serve and that's that."

She stared at him, incredulous. "What?"

"It's going to be too dangerous."

"Phooey. Do you think a couple of little holes in a window are going to stop me from doing what the Lord wants?"

"Don't be ridiculous. God has nothing to do with all this."

"Oh, no? Don't you believe in God?"

"Sure, I do. I'm as good a foxhole Christian as the next guy. But I don't think God is managing my whole life. That's what He gave us brains for."

Julie Ann shook her head and faced him, her lips pressed into a thin line, her hands fisted on her hips.

"Look, *Mr.* Burnett, I appreciate your concern, really I do, but if the Good Lord had not wanted me on this jury, I wouldn't have been chosen. Period. End of discussion."

She yanked open the courthouse door before Smith could do it for her and stomped in ahead of him. She'd had her fill of being told what to do by her overbearing father. She'd been making her own choices for a long time. Good choices. Sane choices.

Praise the Lord she hadn't been right about Smith's amorous interest in her in the past, she added, a bit surprised by the thought. He might have many sterling attributes but he was also the kind of stubborn, domineering man she'd never allow herself to become romantically involved with, no matter what.

Naturally, her Southern upbringing and the fact that Smith was a close friend of Ben's precluded any behavior other than absolute politeness. That did not mean, however, that she was going to be all sugary and sweet to him from now on. The gall of the man, ordering her to use the vandalism as an excuse to back out of serving on the jury.

If anything, the holes in her shop window were all the more reason why she was intent on doing her sworn duty, even if Sherilyn wasn't able to pull herself together and come back to work after their fright.

As she entered the courtroom and took her seat in the jury box, however, Julie Ann was already having second thoughts. No matter how hard she tried to reason away the attack, someone seemed to have it in for her. Someone right here in Serenity. And the first indication of that had come right after she'd been chosen for this jury.

By the end of the first day, three men and four women had been approved by both the prosecuting and defense attorneys, though Smith had not yet been interviewed. He left the courthouse in time to watch Julie Ann dart across the street and pause long enough to unlock the front door of her salon. Someone, probably Harlan, had stuck silver duct tape over the breaks in the window. It wasn't pretty but it seemed an adequate temporary fix.

Hesitating, Smith removed his blazer and slung it over his shoulder by one finger while he tried to decide what to do next. That woman wasn't rational about life in general and her vulnerability in particular. Still, what could he do? He supposed he could follow her home and try to keep an eye on her from a distance.

"And get myself arrested for stalking," Smith muttered to himself, thoroughly disgusted. "Ben would laugh his head off."

Nevertheless, he crossed the street and circled to the rear of the salon, expecting to catch Julie Ann leaving and at least caution her again when she locked up for the day. There was one fairly new, two-door compact car parked there on a gravel pad.

He stared. Circled the parked vehicle to check further. Then, he did the only logical thing, he banged on the back door of the beauty salon with his fist.

When Julie Ann responded, he merely stepped out of the way and gestured toward the car.

She burst through the door like a shot. "My car! What happened?"

"Beats me." Smith stood back, frowning. "Looks like somebody flattened all your tires. Has this ever happened before?"

"No. Never. They were fine when I used this door earlier. At least I think they were." She stared at him. "What are you doing here?"

"I was planning to talk some sense into you and then make sure you got home safely."

"Why?"

"It just seemed like the right thing to do." He wasn't about to admit he'd begun hanging around her more as a favor to her brother and fellow Marine than because he'd actually wanted to. This task had long since progressed past that. It was his duty to look after Julie Ann. That was all there was to it.

"I'll wait right here. Go call Harlan again," Smith said.

To his relief, she ducked back inside and quickly reemerged carrying a portable phone. Smith listened as she did what he'd suggested, then hung up.

"The sheriff says he'll be right over," Julie Ann told him with a sigh and shake of her head as she stared at the damage. "I can't believe this is happening to me."

"Neither can I." He paused, thoughtful. "I wonder if Harlan has had any other odd reports since the jury selection began."

"I'd thought of that possible connection, too. Do you suppose this is all happening because of the trial?"

"It's the only thing I can think of that's changed in the past twenty-four hours."

"I hope you're wrong."

Smith nodded sagely. "I hope so, too." He looked up as the sheriff's black-and-white vehicle cruised slowly into the alley and stopped next to Julie Ann's car.

As Harlan got out and hitched up his gun belt, Smith decided that the portly man looked more serious than he had after they'd turned up no suspects from the first call.

The sheriff circled the vandalized car, then used his radio to request a tow truck before addressing Julie Ann.

"I'm sorry, Miz Julie," Harlan said. "I'll need to take your car in and get it looked at. I think the tires are okay but I'm hoping the perpetrator left fingerprints when he messed with 'em. It's worth a closer look." He glanced at Smith. "Will you be able to see the lady home or shall I have my deputy, Boyd, do it?"

"I'll give her a lift," Smith said before Julie Ann had time to object.

"Good." Harlan looked from one to the other, settling his sober gaze on Julie Ann. "I want you to be real careful, ma'am. I'd feel a lot better if you wasn't alone too much, if you get my drift."

"I live alone, Sheriff," she countered. "And I like it that way. Thank you for your concern but I can look after myself. I'll be fine."

Smith wasn't anywhere near satisfied. "Okay, Harlan. What else is bothering you?"

"Besides the shooter at lunchtime you mean?" He sighed noisily, seeming reluctant to go on. Finally he said, "There was an accident up on Route 9 a little while ago. The steering failed on Estelle Finnerty's car and she plowed into a ditch. She's okay but she was pretty shaken up."

Julie Ann gasped. "Estelle was chosen for Lester's jury today—just like me."

"That looks an awful lot like a pattern to me," Smith said, taking note of Julie Ann's worried look. Now that Harlan had confirmed their suspicions that jurors were being targeted, she'd have to inform the judge.

His fists clenched. If logic didn't get through that thick skull of hers pretty soon, he didn't know what he'd do, but somebody had to do something.

She must have seen the change in his expression because her eyes narrowed. "What?"

"It's like this," Smith said. "There's a fair chance that somebody is trying to frighten jurors—or worse—and you need to take that threat more seriously than you have been so far."

"I'm supposed to be scared of flat tires?"

"No. You're supposed to be worried about bullet holes. Watch yourself like the sheriff says. Go stay with a friend till he can catch whoever's behind all this."

"I'll do nothing of the kind."

"That's what I was afraid of," Smith said. "In that case, you'd better get used to me or Harlan or Boyd being parked outside your house all night."

"Don't be ridiculous. You can't sleep in your car."

"I will if you force me to."

"And you call *me* stubborn."

Suddenly, the hairs on the back of Smith's neck began to prickle. He tensed, quickly scanning the area. There was no one visible except Harlan and Julie Ann, but still…

His gaze met hers. "You feel it, too, don't you?"

"I don't know what you're talking about," she insisted, although she folded her arms across her chest as if she were chilly in spite of the warm temperature.

"I think we're being watched," Smith said.

Harlan reacted immediately. "Both of you get in my car and wait while I lock up for Miz Julie Ann. I'll order a drive-by patrol for here and for her house."

Smith helped Julie Ann into the front seat of the sheriff's car. He'd started to close the door when movement on the shop's roof caught his eye. It was just a fleeting shadow, yet it impressed him as being the size and shape of a grown man. A potential sniper. Just like the ones he'd encountered so often in battle.

Glare from the setting sun over the top of the block building made Smith's eyes water as he shaded them and tried to make out more details.

He had almost convinced himself that his imagination was working too hard until he looked at Julie Ann. Her hazel eyes were wide, her expression revealing. She was clearly afraid. And she was no longer trying to hide or deny it.

For the first time since she'd inherited the old, isolated farm, Julie Ann wasn't happy to be coming home. The pastures which lay to the sides and back of her white-painted frame house seemed too wide and desolate. And the forest of oak, hickory and cedar flanking them was filled with dark, forbidding shadows. If she felt this uneasy in daylight, how was she going to feel once the sun set?

"Are you sure you don't want me to come in and check the house for you?" Smith asked as he pulled into the circular, gravel driveway and stopped. "I don't mind."

Julie Ann almost said yes before she gritted her teeth and shook her head. She was *not* going to give in to irrational fear. And she certainly was not going to let Smith think she needed babysitting.

"No, thanks. That won't be necessary," she told him. "I have an enormous dog inside. He's very protective. If anybody gets past my Andy, they belong here."

Smith started to get out just the same, so she insisted. "I said, I'll be fine."

Though he didn't look convinced, he did back off. "Okay. I'll watch till I see that you're safely inside. And lock the door."

Satisfied that that was as good as the situation was likely to get, she climbed out of the SUV and paused for a moment, hoping her shaking knees weren't going to give her away. "Okay. Thanks for the ride."

"You're quite welcome. I still wish you'd let me…"

Dismissing Smith with a shake of her head, she reached the porch quickly and without faltering. The instant she opened the door and was greeted by her dogs, she relaxed. Thank goodness she was a sucker for sad eyes, cold noses and floppy ears.

Julie Ann turned in the doorway and waved, waiting till Smith had driven off to close the door. Both her dogs had apparently sensed her unusual anxiety because they were acting apprehensive, each in its own way.

Big, stalwart Andy, the black Labrador-Shepherd crossbreed, stationed himself right inside the front door.

Bubbles, a nondescript, dusty-colored mop of dog hair with an attitude, ran loops through the house before leaping and landing next to Julie Ann when she plopped onto the couch.

She ruffled the dog's wiry hair. "I'm glad to see you, too, girl."

Panting and looking very pleased with herself, Bubbles wiggled in response to her master's voice, wagging the entire rear half of her stubby little body.

Julie Ann sighed. "I wish you could talk. Then again, maybe it's just as well you can't. I've had plenty of unasked-for advice already today."

Picturing Smith Burnett's handsome face, she felt comforted yet penitent for being so gruff with him when she knew he was merely trying to help. The fact that he had volunteered to stand guard all night, if need be, made her feel better even though she had sent him away. Any possible source of tranquility was nice to ponder, especially given the kind of day she'd had.

Bubbles jumped down, circled the sofa at a run and bunched a throw rug into a pile when she cut a sharp corner in and out of the archway leading to the country kitchen.

"I know. You're hungry. Come on. Let's go see what we can find for you to eat."

Julie Ann rose and started to cross the small living room. She sensed Andy's bulk at her side before she reached the tiled kitchen floor and heard the click of his nails on the vinyl. He seemed to be mirroring her restless mood a lot more than the other dog. She didn't mind one bit. The closer he crowded, the better she liked it.

She laid her hand atop his broad, dark head and petted him without having to bend down. "Yes, you too, you big lummox. What would I do without my furry buddies?"

Andy's cold nose nudged her hand in response to the loving tone. Julie Ann knew her dogs couldn't understand every word but she also knew they weren't totally clueless.

Picking up their food dishes, she mixed softer food into hard kibble, then set both dishes on the floor the way she always did.

Bubbles immediately dug in. Andy, however, approached his dish as if he were expecting the food to bite him back.

"It's okay, boy. Go ahead. Eat."

Still, the big, black dog refused. He tensed. The hackles on his back rose and Julie Ann heard a throaty growl begin to rumble deep in his chest. Bubbles was impressed enough to pause and glance at him but only for a moment.

Heart racing, Julie Ann scanned the kitchen. Nothing looked out of place. "What is it? What's the matter, Andy?"

The dog was staring at the back door the way a hungry wolf eyed a juicy meal. Had she locked that door? Of course not. She didn't usually bother with such silly precautions. Nothing had ever happened in Serenity to make her fearful or to cause her to change her habits. Until today.

Andy's low, menacing growl continued. Julie Ann thought she saw the doorknob turn. She froze. Her breath caught and she held it, hoping, praying that her overactive imagination was responsible.

No. The knob actually *was* turning. What now? What should she do? If she ran to the door, would she have time to throw the dead bolt? And even if she accomplished that, would it be enough deterrent, or would it merely make her prowler mad and cause him to force his way inside?

Time stood still. Julie Ann's whole body was trembling. So was Andy's. What began as another growl ended as a deep, warning bark. The movement of the knob ceased.

That was enough incentive for Julie Ann. She lunged toward the door.

Andy, barking louder in response to her affirmative actions, was right beside her. Even Bubbles finally joined in with rapid yaps and frantic, scrambling dashes back and forth across the slick kitchen floor.

Julie Ann put out her hand. Grabbed the dead bolt. Twisted it locked.

Just then, the doorknob quivered and made a half turn. Julie Ann knew she'd locked the door just in time because if she had not acted, whoever was outside would now be standing in her kitchen, facing her.

By this time, Andy was in full attack mode. Barking and growling, he hit the wooden door with his front feet, making the whole thing shake.

Julie Ann didn't try to stop or restrain the dog. She wanted her prowler to be good and scared, hopefully enough that he'd go away or at least answer when she shouted, "Who's there?"

All noise and movement suddenly ceased. Andy cocked his head. His ears lifted. Then, he suddenly wheeled and raced back to the living room with Bubbles in scatterbrained, halfhearted pursuit.

By the time Julie Ann realized the new avenue of threat, her protective dog was already barking at the front door, once again ready to defend her.

Smith had told her to lock that door. Had she? She didn't remember. And now Andy was clearly warning her. How long would it take a person to circle her house and reach the front porch? Longer than it took her to go directly there from the kitchen, she reasoned. But not *that* much longer.

With trembling hands and a shaky grip, she engaged the locking mechanism on that door, then proceeded to the windows that were the easiest to access from the porch and secured them, as well.

She hadn't actually spotted anyone prowling outside but they were there just the same. She felt it. And once the sun set, she wouldn't be able to see any farther than the circles of illumination cast by her porch lights.

Andy stayed close beside her every step of the way, often so near that she had to nudge him aside to reach the windows.

"What's this world coming to when a person has to lock everything just to feel safe?" she muttered.

Andy's only response was to nuzzle her hand.

She paused just long enough to give him another pat, then finished with the windows that sat higher off the ground than a man could normally reach. If her prowler had a ladder and tried to open one of those, he'd be thwarted then, too.

The whole scenario was beginning to make her

angry. How dare anyone try to get into her home? How dare they frighten her this way? She didn't deserve to have her salon window broken or her tires flattened, and she certainly wasn't going to allow herself to become a further victim. Not if she could help it.

Grabbing her phone she dialed the emergency number. Instead of the part-time dispatcher she had expected, Harlan answered the call.

"Sheriff's office."

Julie Ann was surprised to hear his voice.

"It's me. Julie Ann Jones," she said, gripping the phone tightly. "There's a prowler outside my house."

"What makes you think so?"

His question was irksome. "Because the dog is barking, the door rattled and the knob turned, only nobody said a word when I hollered at them. Isn't that enough?"

"It'll do," the sheriff answered. "Sit tight and stay inside. I'll send Boyd right over."

"Okay." Julie Ann nodded as she ended the call. Her brain had been spinning wildly during the crisis but she was now thinking more clearly. As long as she was stuck in an isolated house at least a half mile from her nearest neighbor, she was far too vulnerable. Harlan had only one full-time deputy and the county owned two patrol cars. Period. How much time could he and Boyd afford to devote to looking after her? Very little, especially since her farm was so far out of town.

She had only two choices, she decided easily. She'd either have to phone Smith and admit she needed protecting or go to Grandpa Willis's trunk, dig through the personal items he had willed her when he'd died, and find the revolver they had shared when he'd taught her how to shoot.

As much as she hated the idea of running around the house armed like a gunslinger from a western movie, she wasn't going to just sit there and become a helpless victim.

And she certainly was not going to phone Smith Burnett and admit she needed protection, particularly his. She was a country girl, born and raised. She could take care of herself. At least she hoped she could.

FOUR

Smith was still concerned and thinking about Julie Ann when he drove past his office near the town square. A sheriff's car, lights flashing and siren wailing, raced by him going the opposite direction. His heart leaped and felt as if it were lodged in his throat. The patrol car was heading in the direction of Julie Ann's!

He tried to shrug off his misgivings, found he couldn't, and decided to make a U-turn and follow. If he got as far as her neighborhood and didn't spot the police, he'd go on home and try to forget he'd been so impulsive. The last thing he needed was to have her so mad at him for disregarding her wishes that she purposely tried to thwart his efforts to look after her.

As he rounded the final bend on Squirrel Hill Road and glanced up at the hillside, his breath caught. The rotating beacons of the blue and red lights were right in front of Julie Ann's house.

What'd happened to her?

Smith accelerated and began to drive as if he were racing against an unseen nemesis. Thank goodness his SUV was built to take the punishment of pothole-filled, rock-strewn, dirt roads. His hands held the wheel in a death grip. His jaw clenched. He should never have left her without insisting he check that house first. *Never*. No matter how much she'd protested against it.

As he skidded to a stop behind the sheriff's car, he spotted two figures standing in the shadows. He bailed out, ready to do battle. Julie Ann was easy to recognize but the tall, skinny guy with her had better have a very good reason to be there.

Jogging toward the porch, Smith realized that the other man was Harlan's deputy. That did little to relieve his disgust with himself for leaving Julie Ann alone and his anger at her for insisting she'd be fine.

"What happened?" Smith immediately demanded, shouting in order to be heard over the noisy barking coming from inside the house.

Boyd shook his head and answered. "Don't rightly know. Miz Jones thought she had a prowler. Nobody was around when I got here."

"Considering your lights and siren, that's not too surprising," Smith grumbled. He stared at her. "You okay?"

"Fine. Why did you come back?"

"I saw the police car driving this way."

"What made you think it was headed out here?"

"Gut feelings." Smith raked his fingers through his hair. "I just took a chance, okay? After everything else that's happened today it was a reasonable conclusion."

She seemed to accept that explanation, yet Smith could tell she was not totally convinced that he needed to be there. "What do I have to do to make you believe you're in danger?" he asked.

"There's no need to worry about me," Julie Ann replied. "I can take care of myself."

"Oh? It doesn't look like it to me."

The gangly deputy agreed. "That's what I was tellin' her when you drove up. Maybe you can talk some sense into her." He touched the brim of his hat in parting. "Well, there's nothing more I can do here. If you see anybody who looks funny, you give us another call, ma'am."

Smith stepped aside to let Boyd pass, then rejoined Julie Ann. "I want to know everything. Tell me what happened." When she turned slightly and he saw that she was wearing a sidearm in an old leather holster, he pointed and said exactly what he was thinking. "Good grief, woman. Where did you get *that?*"

"It was my grandpa's." Her hand rested on the ivory grip but she gave no indication that she was going to draw the pistol to show it to him.

"And that's why you think you'll be safe?" Smith huffed in disparagement. "You're more likely to hurt yourself with that thing."

"Grandpa Willis taught me how to shoot. I know what I'm doing."

"Suppose somebody takes it away from you and turns the tables? What then?"

She scowled. "You're just full of wonderful ideas, aren't you?"

"I'm being sensible. You can't go around like Annie Oakley. Haven't you ever heard of Mace or a Taser gun?"

"Sure, I have. I just don't happen to have either in my closet and I did have this gun. Under the circumstances, it seemed like a good idea to get it out and load it."

Smith gestured toward the porch swing and spoke as calmly as he could. "Will you please sit down and talk to me? I really would like to know what happened."

When she hesitated, he added a second "Please?"

"All right. As soon as I let Andy and Bubbles out so they don't bark themselves hoarse or beat down the door. If Andy thinks you're okay, we'll talk."

Her attitude was off-putting. "Then I sure hope he likes me because I intend to hang around until I hear your whole story."

To Smith's relief, Julie Ann didn't just fling open the front door and let her mammoth dog charge out to attack. She spoke to Andy calmly, then put one hand on his collar and escorted him to meet her guest while the much smaller mutt ran in rapid circles on the porch, panting excitedly with its nose to the ground as if hot on the trail of a wild rabbit.

Andy eased up to Smith, sniffed his shoes and pants legs, then ducked his broad, black head under the man's hand as if greeting a trustworthy old friend.

Wiggling his fingers slightly, Smith scratched the dog's velvety ears. "I think I get to stay."

"Looks like it," Julie Ann said with a surprised expression.

"You didn't think we'd get along?"

"Actually, no. Andy was abused by his former owner. He doesn't usually take to strangers."

"I see. Well, since your excuse for ordering me to leave is gone, now what?"

"We talk." Adjusting the holster for comfort, she chose a seat at one end of the hanging porch swing and gestured to the empty place. "Since you're already here, I suppose I may as well go ahead and fill you in on the details. Then we can check around back for clues."

"Boyd didn't look?"

She shook her head slowly and pressed her lips into a thin line. "Nope. I guess he assumed I was just a panic-stricken woman who imagined a prowler because I was too high-strung."

"Did you actually see anyone?"

"No. But Andy was sure there was someone on the back porch."

"Could he have been mistaken?"

Shivers ran up Smith's neck when she answered, "Not unless doorknobs turn all by themselves."

Julie Ann did her best to relate the most recent events in a way that sounded calm and self-assured. If she hadn't sensed Smith's growing tension as she spoke, she might have thought she'd been successful at masking her own fear. Now that the supposed danger was past, she did feel a bit silly for having been so frightened.

"So, after I called the sheriff, I dug out Grandpa's old pistol. I don't intend to take it to work but it did seem like a pretty good idea to keep it handy here. At least until I figure out what's going on."

Seeming to sense her continued anxiety, Andy wagged his tail and laid his chin on her lap.

"If I'd heard that big moose barking inside your house, I sure wouldn't have opened the door." Smith stood. "Why don't you put the dogs up while I grab a flashlight from my truck? Then we'll walk around back and check it out."

"Do you really think we might find tracks or something?"

"I hope not," Smith said. "But if we do, I intend to phone Harlan myself and tell him what I think of his deputy's careless treatment of a crime scene."

Julie Ann led Andy and Bubbles to the screen door and ushered them inside, firmly closing the heavier, paneled door while Smith went to fetch the flashlight.

"Nothing actually happened," she said when he returned.

"Only by the grace of God."

Agreeing but not commenting, Julie Ann followed him off the porch and around the side of the house. Truth to tell, if Smith had not been beside her, she would have gone back into the house with Andy and locked the doors again instead of proceeding into the shadowy depths of her garden.

The enormous hydrangea at the corner of the porch was merely an innocent plant. She knew that as well as she knew her own name, yet its leaves seemed to flutter and reach for her like grasping hands. The shade trees cast creepy, moonlit shadows on the lawn. A whip-poor-will's call sounded plaintive and eerie. Every normally innocent sound or sight made her tense up as if she were about to be attacked.

Her palm rested atop the pistol grip. She didn't know if she could actually shoot anyone who threatened her but she wasn't going to hesitate to bluff if the need arose.

When Smith put out his arm to block her forward movement, she almost ran into him. "What?"

He pointed the flashlight beam. "If those are your footprints, you have a lot bigger feet than I thought."

Staring at the imprints, she gasped. Her mouth was suddenly so dry she couldn't swallow. "I—I don't wear boots with a waffle sole. I never have."

"That's what I was afraid of."

Smith reached into his pocket and took out a cell phone. Julie Ann hugged herself and listened while he made a call to Harlan and explained what they'd found.

As soon as he hung up, she asked "Is he sending Boyd back?" The disgusted expression on Smith's face answered her question even before he spoke.

"No. They're busy with an accident out on the highway. No one's available."

She saw him tilt his head to eye the sky and noticed that the previously clear evening was starting to look suspiciously cloudy. "Do you think it's going to rain before they can get here?"

"Knowing Arkansas, that's a strong probability. Especially this time of year. Can you think of any way we can shelter those prints to preserve them?"

"I suppose we could put a box or something like that over them but if the rain is heavy, it'll probably wash the whole thing away." Frustrated, she clenched her fists. "Nobody believes me. I tell them there's a prowler and nobody believes me."

"I do," Smith said.

Julie Ann sensed the truth of his statement though she could not clearly see his face. Of course, they were standing there staring at proof in the narrow beam of light so it wasn't exactly a stretch for him to vouch for her veracity. Still, she was grateful. "Thanks."

"You're welcome. Go see if you can find a box bigger than one of these prints and I'll fetch a couple of rocks to hold it down in case we get wind with the rain."

"This is going to be hopeless and you know it."

"The only way to be sure we'll fail is to not try," Smith countered.

"You don't think the Lord will protect the prints if they're that important?"

"No more than you believe He will protect you."

"But I do believe He will," she insisted, standing her ground and daring him to argue.

Smith gave her a lopsided smile and shrugged. "Really? Then take off that gun and prove it."

Less than an hour after Smith had finally left, at her insistence, the torrential rains began. Sheet lightning repeatedly lit the sky from horizon to horizon and driving winds hurled sheets of water against the old frame house so violently that the windowpanes vibrated.

Storms like this one had made Julie Ann terribly nervous since childhood. Add that to her already edgy mood tonight and she was about to jump out of her skin. Every flash of light, every rumble of thunder increased her alarm, and no amount of rational argument could banish it.

Pacing, hugging herself, she hoped that the electricity wouldn't fail. If it did, she'd have to decide whether to swelter in a house with no air conditioning or open a few windows and make another assault easier.

Going to bed and sleeping was out of the question. She finally grabbed the remote and switched on the TV. It didn't matter what was playing. All she wanted was the company of human voices and enough background noise to help drown out the raging storm.

Thankful that Smith wasn't there to see how unduly anxious she was, she plopped down on the sofa and cuddled up with Bubbles while Andy lay at her feet. It had belatedly occurred to her that if she were actually threatened and Andy went to her aid, there was a chance the faithful dog would be hurt. She could never allow that to happen.

"Could I shoot an attacker?" she asked herself for the umpteenth time. "Probably not." Maybe Smith had been right when he'd suggested that wielding the pistol wasn't a wise choice. Then again, it beat standing here defenseless and letting someone kill her the way Denny apparently had been.

That thought brought tears to her eyes. She wasn't ready to give up on this life just yet. She was still young, still had so much ahead of her. For one thing, she'd hoped to one day become a mother and have a bunch of children.

Snorting derisively, Julie Ann made a face as her thoughts came full circle. Unless she chose to adopt, there was no way to fulfill her dream without first finding a husband.

The image of Smith Burnett popped into her head immediately. She tried to will it away. When that failed, she turned to prayer, which she realized should have been her first choice, not her last resort.

"Father, forgive me for being scared," she began. "I know I should be trusting You more. And I want to. I really do. I just can't help how I feel."

The scripture in II Timothy came to her. "For God has not given us a spirit of fear, but of power and of love and of a sound mind."

That was the crux of her problem, Julie Ann decided. She knew God loved her and had gifted her with the wits to outsmart her enemies when she knew who or what she was up against. It was being powerless in the face of invisible forces that left her shaking.

"I wish…"

Stopping herself from voicing the thought, she nevertheless completed it in her mind. She wished Smith were still there, still acting as her protector.

"Dear Lord, what's the matter with me?" she prayed, fighting tears. "I've already ruined any chance he and I may have had by throwing myself at him when I was seventeen. Besides, he's way too much like my dad."

Julie Ann reached for a tissue and blew her nose. There might be no way to alter the past but that didn't mean it had to control or ruin her future. It was good to know that Smith was her friend even though that was all they might ever be to each other. He was a good man. An honest man. A person she was proud to know. And besides being grateful that he was back in Serenity, she was also glad that he and Ben had become such good friends. Smith's steadying influence had helped her brother break free of bad company and had led him to a military career that had finished the job of making sure he became a fine man.

And? Her jaw clenched. And nothing. That was all there was to her relationship with Smith. All there ever could be. Turning back to her impromptu prayer she thanked the Lord for all the people in her life, for her friends and family, then asked for understanding toward those who apparently hated her.

That concept hurt all the way to her tender soul. She had never done anything to hurt anyone. Why were there evil forces trying to harm her?

"And thank You for bringing Smith back into my life just when I needed him," Julie Ann added in closing. "Please, please keep him safe."

Because I care for him, remained unsaid. It was true. It was also hard to accept, let alone squarely face and deal with. What in the world was wrong with her? Where had her self-confidence gone? And why was she becoming so fond of Smith Burnett all of a sudden? Reacting to stress was one thing. Falling for Smith again was quite another.

Julie Ann had dozed on the sofa until dawn. She had been less astonished than chagrined to discover that the inverted wastebasket she'd placed over the footprint behind her house had failed to keep water from obliterating it.

When she arrived in Serenity the following morning, she saw Smith Burnett standing by the courthouse door and assumed he was waiting for her.

They met halfway across the damp lawn. "Well, it

rained like we thought it would," he said. "How did the prints fare?"

"Poorly. There's not very good drainage in my backyard and the water got too deep."

"I was afraid of that." He eyed her quizzically. "I see you left your Annie Oakley gun at home."

"Yes. It's locked away again. I figured it would attract way too much attention if I tried to wear it into the courthouse."

"And probably get you arrested. We have to pass through a metal detector, remember?"

She made a face. "I was joking. I didn't intend to really do it. Now that I think about it, though, it might make a good deterrent."

"That's a matter of opinion."

"Exactly. Mine," she said flatly.

As she started toward the courthouse, Smith fell into step beside her. "I phoned your house this morning to see if you needed a ride but you must have already left. When did you get your car back?"

"Harlan and Boyd had the tires pumped up and brought it to me late last night, after the storm," she said as he reached to open the door.

Although her first instinct was to forge ahead and do it herself, she couldn't bring herself to purposely deny him his natural expression of Southern manners. Yes, she was able to take care of herself. And, yes, she could certainly open a door without a man's help. But Smith was behaving so gallantly it touched her conscience.

Her late teens and early twenties had taught her that self-reliance was vital for the survival of her personality, her very soul. Nothing had happened since to change her mind, she had merely become more mature about insisting upon doing everything her own way.

She preceded Smith up the stairs to the courtroom, then left him to take her place in the jury box. Seventy-year-old Estelle Finnerty was already there, as were the other jurors who had already been chosen. The opposing attorneys, Grimes for the prosecution and Lazarus for the defense, had files spread out on their respective tables.

Lester Taney, wearing the familiar bright orange prison jumpsuit, sat off to one side. Julie Ann did her best to avoid giving him more than a cursory glance. The gray-haired, unshaven, old man was the picture of dejection, yet she knew she should not make any decisions about his guilt or innocence merely because she felt sorry for him. Which she did. To take someone's life was a terrible sin. Then again, as she had already concluded, a wrongful conviction would be terrible, too.

As soon as the judge entered, the proceedings got under way and more jurors were seated before Smith Burnett was called to the front.

Julie Ann's heartbeat increased and she had to fold her hands in her lap to keep from fidgeting as she watched him stand, button his jacket and square his shoulders before going forward.

She knew Smith didn't want to be chosen to serve on the jury but in her heart of hearts she wanted him there. She had a passing acquaintance with each of the other jurors. Nevertheless, she desperately wanted Smith to be assigned to join them.

"And is there any reason why you cannot serve, Mr. Burnett?" Grimes asked after completing the first formalities, including questions about Smith's possible acquaintance with the principals involved.

"I have a real estate business to run," Smith answered, glancing at the judge. "We're heading into my busiest season and it will be a real hardship for me to be away from work. It already is."

"How much time do you spend in your office each day?" the attorney asked.

Julie Ann could tell that Smith was struggling with his conscience. Finally, he said, "About four," then quickly added, "but the rest of the time I'm out showing properties or getting listings."

"Who watches your office when you're out?"

Sighing, Smith said, "I'm the licensed broker. I have a part-time salesperson who also answers the phones and sometimes helps with paperwork."

As he concluded, his gaze rested on Julie Ann. She nodded in commiseration, trying to hide her relief when the judge got the defense's okay and then said, "Take a seat in the jury box, Mr. Burnett."

Though Smith couldn't sit directly beside her because those chairs were already occupied, she was still overjoyed. It was selfish but she couldn't help having that gut reaction. There was something terribly reassuring about being in his company, knowing that he was around, even though he was so bossy most of the time that he drove her crazy.

She smiled to herself. No doubt Smith would find it less than amusing to hear that she felt that way about

Andy, too. And since the judge would undoubtedly frown on her bringing either her big dog or her gun to court for comfort, having Smith there was the next best thing.

FIVE

By the end of that afternoon, all twelve jurors and two alternates had been chosen. Smith waited at the exit for Julie Ann while others filed past him. When he saw her sheepish expression he was puzzled.

"What's up? You look kind of funny."

"Sorry. Guilty conscience, I guess." She gave him a slight smile.

"What for? Did you chew gum in court or something?"

"No. I just feel bad for feeling good."

Smith escorted her out into the late afternoon sunshine and shaded his eyes with one hand. "You've totally lost me."

"Okay, I'll confess. I know you didn't want to be picked to serve but I was glad when you were."

"Care to tell me why?"

She huffed. "It surprised me as much as it seems to have surprised you. I guess it's because you helped me twice."

"Actually, it was three times so far," Smith said, "if you count the shooting, the flat tires and the footprints last night."

"I stand corrected. Three times it is. I hope that's the end of it."

"So do I. Now that the jury selection is over, do you suppose others will begin to have problems, too?"

"I guess it's possible." She looked around the square as their fellow jurors dispersed. "Should we try to warn them?"

"And say what? That Harlan and Boyd think we're both crazy for taking the vandalism so seriously?"

"It may have been more than just me," Julie Ann said, cupping her hand around her mouth and leaning closer to him to speak in secret. "Estelle says she doesn't know why her steering failed and she ran into that ditch."

"Did Harlan look at her car?"

"She says he was going to. It was towed to the Serenity Repair Shop. She doesn't know if anybody found anything wrong with it."

Smith paused, scowling. "When Harlan brought you your car, did he say whether they'd lifted any fingerprints?"

"Yes. There was nothing. The fender was clean as a whistle. He and Boyd offered to look at the footprints we found, but it was too late to see anything useful by the time they got there last night. Too much mud." She sighed. "He said we should have taken digital pictures. I never thought of doing that. Did you?"

"No."

"I suppose I was too nervous to think clearly."

"How are you feeling now?" Smith asked, truly concerned but trying to sound as nonchalant as possible. He had worried about Julie Ann all night and had almost driven back to her place more than once.

In retrospect, he was thankful that he had not, especially since Harlan and his deputy had dropped by to deliver her car. If either of them had caught him out there again they might have gotten the wrong idea. In a small community like Serenity, rumors were more than the spice of life—they were the meat and potatoes, too.

"So, Ms. Jones, what are your plans for the rest of the day?"

"I'm going to stop in and see how Sherilyn is coping, then cancel the rest of my appointments for this week. Do you think I should include next week's, too?"

"Probably, although I don't believe this trial will take very long. Certainly not as long as one in a big city would." He frowned. "I was amazed that the lawyers didn't ask for a change of venue. Everybody in town knows Lester, at least in some way."

"I think we'll be fair to him, though. Don't you?"

"As long as some of those softhearted church ladies don't give him a break he doesn't deserve," Smith said flatly.

"I beg your pardon?"

Judging by the astonishment on her face and the tinge of rancor in her tone, he'd been too outspoken. Too bad there was no way to take back his opinion. "You know what I mean. Some people tend to give everyone the benefit of a doubt even when evidence of guilt is clear as day."

"You've already decided Lester's guilty, haven't you?"

"Of course not. I just think…"

"Well, I don't. And if that makes me too soft, so be it. I'd rather be considered kind than mean-spirited."

"I wasn't accusing you of anything like that."

"Oh? It sure sounded like it to me."

"If the shoe fits…"

"Exactly," Julie Ann interrupted, her hands fisted on her hips, her spine stiff.

Smith tried to mask his exasperation. "You might want to try to separate yourself from your role as a juror and remember that I am not your enemy, *Ms.* Jones." He paused and studied her sparkling hazel eyes and stony expression, looking for some glimmer of understanding. "Believe it or not, I'm on your side."

She softened visibly. "I know that. I just don't want anybody to think I'm biased one way or the other. And you shouldn't give that impression, either. Not unless you truly want to be disqualified."

"No," he said, shaking his head. "I'll serve. We both will. I just want you to know that outside of court I'd like to be your friend." He chanced a slight smile. "I kind of thought I already was."

"Friends accept each other as they are. They don't try to change the other person," Julie Ann replied.

"I can't agree more. You're absolutely right."

Smith's smile grew into a grin of satisfaction that became a laugh when she gave him a cynical look and added, "Except in the case of stubborn men like you who happen to be dead wrong and won't admit it."

As the trial got under way, Julie Ann felt relieved, knowing that this nightmare of responsibility would soon be over and her life could get back to normal.

She had to force herself to concentrate through the attorneys' preliminary statements, however, because there were several casual observers seated in the courtroom whose presence made the hair on the back of her neck prickle.

The most notable were two scowling, elderly men who looked slightly familiar, although she couldn't think of their names. She considered asking one of the older jurors if he knew them, then decided against it. It would be natural for Lester's friends and contemporaries to attend his trial. That was probably who those men were and why their mood seemed so dour.

She would have felt better about it if they hadn't kept staring at the jury box, though. There were times when she'd felt as if they were glaring directly at her, daring her to convict and issuing unspoken threats if she even considered doing so.

Poor Denny's grandmother, Margaret Hanford, was seated in the front row of the gallery. Julie Ann had attended church with Miss Margaret for years. She sympathized with the gray-haired woman's personal loss. Everything about her exemplified the terrible trauma she had suffered, from her reddened eyes which she kept dabbing with a tissue, to the slump of her thin shoulders.

Harlan took the stand to describe the scene of the killing.

Julie Ann listened carefully while peeking surreptitiously at the old men who seemed so angry and intent. They hadn't done or said one thing out of line, yet their demeanor made her skin crawl and her hands grow clammy.

When she saw one nod and draw closer to the other, then cup his hand around the corner of his mouth and apparently share something in confidence, she held her breath. They were both looking directly at her.

If she hadn't already been so on edge, she might not have jumped when Smith tapped her on the shoulder and leaned forward from his seat in the row directly behind her.

"It's just me," he whispered. "Are you okay?"

Julie Ann's heart was pounding. Nevertheless, she nodded.

"You see them sitting out there, too, don't you?"

Another nod. She was watching the judge, hoping he wouldn't notice that she and Smith were in contact during the proceedings. She wasn't sure if that was a no-no but couldn't imagine that it was allowed.

She turned her head slightly and felt Smith's warm breath on her cheek as she asked, "Do you know who they are?"

"No," he said softly. "Do you?"

She shook her head, the movement barely perceptible. "They do seem familiar."

"I thought so, too."

Just then, Elwin Grimes, the prosecuting attorney who had been questioning Harlan, turned and stared at the jury box so pointedly that Smith sat back and Julie Ann blushed. Though he didn't address anyone individually, he did ask the judge to instruct the entire jury to be quiet and pay closer attention.

Julie Ann was mortified. It was as if she were a teenager and had been caught passing notes or text-messaging a boyfriend during class, although she'd never been in the habit of doing things like that. She had believed, from an early age, that her education was paramount and that social interaction definitely came second. So much so that she'd had very few dates during high school, which was probably another reason why Smith's unexpected offer to escort her to the prom had left her so confused.

It wasn't that Julie Ann was disinterested in dating, it was simply that her priorities had differed from those of most of her peers. And she had decided long ago that she was not going to consider marriage simply as a way to help support herself. She was her own person and wanted everyone to know it.

And now she had a different kind of job to do, she reminded herself. A very important job. One man had died and another was being tried for his murder. Life didn't get any more serious or complicated than that.

Harlan continued from the witness box. "The deceased was found by his car, off Highway 9 at the storage yard. He'd been hit in the chest with a shotgun blast. The coroner says he can tell by the pattern that there were two shots fired."

"We'll speak to him later," Grimes advised. "Just describe the crime scene the way you observed it."

As the sheriff went on adding necessary detail, Julie Ann was deeply touched by Margaret Hanford's grief. It was palpable. Moving and undeniable.

That doesn't mean that Lester is guilty, Julie Ann told herself. If he didn't kill Denny it would be very wrong to blame him, even though doing so would end the trial quickly.

Another thought struck her and made her catch her breath. If Lester was innocent, then who *did* do it? Could it be one of the people so intent on watching the proceedings in person? Or could it have been whoever was apparently targeting jurors like her and Estelle?

A shiver shot up her spine and lifted the fine hairs at her nape. If it was not Lester who had ended the young man's life, then there was still a murderer loose in Serenity. And he might be staring at her that very second!

"Were you in the courtroom today?" Evans asked his cohort.

"Yeah. But I kept a low profile."

"That was wise. What did you hear?"

"It looks like a slam-dunk to me. Lester's got no alibi and all the motive in the world, thanks to us."

"That's not good. I want the trial to drag on as long as possible. Do what you can to prolong it."

The second man huffed. "Don't think I'll have to do much. Some of those dumb locals are doing it for us. So far they haven't made much headway, but they're still scaring the jurors. Even shot out a window and flattened some tires."

"That's child's play. If the trial looks like it's about to end, you'll have to thin the jury, if you get my meaning."

"Permanently or temporarily?"

"I don't care one way or the other. Just keep Lester in Serenity so they can't begin the bootlegging trial in Little Rock. I need at least another month."

"How much of that fresh ethanol can you siphon off

to sell for drinking without getting caught, anyway? I'd think the folks in charge of the NRG plant's output would catch on."

"Not if some of them are paid enough to look the other way when I adjust the totals," Evans answered. "Don't worry about my end of the deal. You just see to it that Lester's trial drags on and hope that none of the other small-time bootleggers we will frame in the future have to be revealed too soon. I want to space them out. You got that?"

"Yeah, yeah. I've got it. I'll drop by a couple of the local hangouts and see what the gossip is. If it doesn't sound like our good old boys are going to get more serious about scaring jurors, I'll step in."

"Good. I knew I could count on you." Evans chuckled, sounding sinister. "Don't forget. It could be your life on the line instead of Lester's."

"Is that a threat?"

"No. Merely a statement of fact. Now go do what I pay you for."

Smith had spent the better part of his morning in court worrying about Julie Ann. He knew he should be concerned about himself, as well as the other jurors, but his thoughts kept returning to the young woman seated in the row in front of him.

He'd been watching her during Harlan's testimony and had seen her shiver more than once. Since the courtroom was warm and she had a sweater draped across her shoulders, he assumed her reaction was due to the appalling nature of the sheriff's descriptions.

That was to be expected, especially since Smith knew Julie Ann had a tender heart. He sincerely hoped that her sentiments were not going to get in the way of a just conviction, however. As far as he was concerned, the old man was "guilty as sin," as the old-timers said. The testimonies of Harlan, Boyd and the county coroner were good enough to convince Smith. Unless Lester Taney had a better alibi than had been presented so far, he had to have been the one who'd killed Denny. Besides the fact that he'd been caught red-handed, no one else had had an adequate motive.

When the jury broke for lunch, Smith had intended to ask Julie Ann to eat with him but some of the women jurors had beat him to it and she'd left with a group of them. As long as she stayed out in public, surrounded by other people, he felt she'd be safe enough. It was the hours she spent alone on the old farm that kept him up nights worrying, and probably would for some time to come.

After lunch, Julie Ann stopped by her shop to check on Sherilyn before returning to the courthouse. "Hi. How are you doing today?"

"Okay."

"You don't look okay." Approaching Sherilyn, Julie Ann laid a reassuring hand on the girl's forearm. "I can understand being scared by the shots through the window. I think it's time you told me why you were so upset the day we heard what happened to Denny."

Sherilyn jerked away. "I don't know what you mean."

"Yes, you do. I've been asking around. Denny and

some of his buddies were seen here more than once, always on the afternoons when I was gone, scheduled to do hair and nails at the rest homes."

"So, a few of my friends stopped by. So what?"

"I warned you about not encouraging visitors before I offered you this job," Julie Ann said. "I understand that you may get bored when I'm gone, but that's no excuse for breaking the rules."

Sherilyn swiped away the tears rolling down her cheeks. "I'm glad I did. Denny was really sweet to me."

The hair at Julie Ann's nape prickled. "Then he *was* here."

"Yes. He loved me. He said so. And now he's..." She buried her face in her hands and burst into sobs.

"Do you have any idea who might have killed him?"

"That—that nasty old man did it. Everybody says so."

"Suppose he didn't. What then? Don't you want to see justice done?" Lowering her voice she asked, "What else can you tell me? What was Denny doing for money these days?"

"He—he never said. But he had a good job. I know he did. He was going to buy a new car and give me his old one so I wouldn't have to walk to work. And he promised to marry me just as soon as he got done with his business deal."

"What business deal? Was he working for Lester Taney?"

"I don't know." The girl wept noisily. "Stop picking on me. I didn't do anything bad. I didn't."

Julie Ann would have pursued their discussion in greater depth but it was time to return to the courtroom.

She handed Sherilyn a box of tissues before leaving. "Okay. That's enough for now. Why don't you put a sign on the door explaining that I have jury duty and take the rest of the afternoon off? You can't sell beauty to other people when you have a red nose and puffy eyes."

"Do you mean it?"

"Yes. Don't worry. I'll pay you your regular salary."

"Th-thanks. And Julie Ann?" She sniffled and swiped at her damp cheeks. "I'm sorry I broke your rules and kept secrets from you. Honest I am."

Hugging the teen, she reassured her before starting for the door. It wasn't that kind of secret that bothered Julie Ann. It was the other secrets, the dangerous ones, that had her so on edge. When senseless murder had come to Serenity, peace and tranquility had vanished the way the predawn mist in the valleys burned off when the sun rose. There was a cold-blooded killer in their midst. And, in her estimation, it was looking less and less likely that it was Lester Taney.

Just as she was stepping off the curb, she was joined by Estelle Finnerty.

"Wait for me!" the elderly woman called. "I'm not as spry as I used to be and I hate to cross alone."

"How are you doing since the accident? Still stiff and sore?"

"Honey, I've been so stiff and sore for years I can hardly tell any difference," Estelle said with an impish grin.

That upbeat attitude toward chronic pain made Julie Ann really admire her. She offered her arm to Estelle and they started to cross together. "I hope the trial is over soon, don't you?"

"I wouldn't care how long it took if they'd let me bring my crocheting along," Estelle said. "Seems like such a waste of time to just sit there. I usually watch my soaps while I make doilies, so I know I can listen just fine."

"I'm sure you can."

Traffic had been sparse as they had stepped off the curb. Julie Ann would already have been safely to the other side of the wide street if she hadn't slowed her pace to match her companion's.

She looked up as she heard an engine roar and tires squeal. A beat-up, tan-colored pickup truck slewed around the corner and accelerated. It was headed right for them!

"Hurry," Julie Ann urged, growing apprehensive. "That idiot is coming awfully fast."

Instead of picking up her pace, the older woman froze and stared.

"Estelle. Let's go!" Julie Ann tugged on her bony arm gently and dragged her, forcing her to shuffle her feet. Julie Ann didn't want to hurt her but they had to get out of the way. Any temporary discomfort was better than the alternative.

Because she was the one backing up and pulling, Julie Ann reached the empty space between two parked cars an instant before Estelle did. If the truck hadn't swerved at the last instant, the old woman would have been safe, too.

Julie Ann screamed and jerked Estelle's arm.

She almost saved her.

The impact of the pickup's fender against Estelle's lower body snatched her from Julie's grasp and threw her into the street.

"No!" Hardly able to believe what had just occurred, Julie Ann fell to her knees beside the other woman's limp body as the truck sped away. "Estelle? Talk to me. Say something," she begged.

A crowd gathered.

A woman in the background screamed.

"Everybody stand back," a bystander yelled.

"Where did that truck go?" someone else asked. "Did anybody get the license number?"

Julie Ann grasped the thin, clammy hand of the victim, holding it gently and checking the wrist for a pulse. It was rapid and thready but Estelle was clearly alive.

"Call an ambulance!" Julie Ann ordered, yelling to make herself heard over the surrounding din. She saw several people immediately raise cell phones.

Harlan Allgood arrived before anyone had had time to finish reporting the accident. He knelt down beside the victim. "Estelle again," he announced, barely glancing at Julie Ann. "Did you see what happened?"

"Yes. I was helping her cross the street. This was no accident. A truck went out of its way to hit her."

"You sure about that?"

It was all Julie Ann could do to keep from screaming at him. "Yes. I'm positive."

"Okay. An ambulance is on its way. I'll take over now."

Just then, another man forced his way through the rear of the throng and shouted, "Julie Ann!" There was no mistaking Smith's voice or his panicky tone.

When she stood and faced him, she was thunder-struck at the distress reflected in his dark eyes.

He stared at her. "I thought… I was afraid it was you."

Reaching toward him she placed her hand on his forearm to offer consolation. "It almost was."

"You're okay?" Smith's voice was low and his words had a telltale tremor.

"I'm fine. We were just coming across the street together when a truck purposely hit Estelle. I tried to pull her out of the way. It was awful."

When Smith moved to embrace her, Julie Ann slipped her arms around his waist and gladly accepted the solace and moral support he offered. There was nothing wrong with a little TLC in a situation like this, she reasoned. Nothing at all. Surely no one would mistake the gesture for anything other than mutual comforting, not even Smith.

Julie Ann shuddered as the truth of the whole incident became clear. She and Estelle had both been crossing the street. It could just as easily have been *her* who was lying unconscious in the street awaiting an ambulance.

It was only by the grace of God that she was unscathed.

In the midst of the chaos she had not even thought of giving thanks. Now, in Smith's embrace, she praised the Lord for her deliverance and asked Him to care for Estelle.

And while she was at it, she added heartfelt thanks for Smith Burnett.

SIX

The Friday afternoon session of Lester's trial was canceled while the authorities investigated Estelle's accident and searched for the unidentified hit-and-run driver of the old, tan truck.

Rather than go home, Julie Ann had returned to her hair salon and scheduled a few quick appointments. Her mood stayed fairly upbeat except when she forgot and glanced at the bullet holes in her window.

Louella Higgins was the first person she'd phoned. The flamboyant matron walked through the shop door half an hour later, hugged Julie Ann, then patted her own reddish curls with a bejeweled hand. "I'm so glad you called. I was starting to worry that I'd have to do my hair myself. You know how that always turns into a fiasco."

Julie Ann led her to the sink and fitted her with a plastic cape before shampooing. "You should be glad I'm even alive, let alone working. Did you hear about the accident this afternoon?"

"Yes! Did you see it happen?"

"I'll say. Estelle and I were crossing the street together when she was hit."

"Oh, my dear. I'm so sorry. Are you okay?"

"I'm coping," Julie Ann said as she worked up a lather. "Between that and everything else that's been going wrong, I'm exhausted. I'd thought Lester's trial would move right along but it's dragging something awful. It took nearly a week to pick the jurors and we've lost one already."

"Poor Estelle. I hope the sheriff catches whoever ran her down."

As Julie Ann wrapped Louella's head in a fresh towel, the older woman continued. "Harlan'll do his best, I know. He may not have all the fancy equipment they have in big city departments, but he manages. After all, he caught Lester and his nephew, didn't he?"

"True." Julie Ann settled her friend at her station, then met her gaze in the wide mirror.

Louella immediately picked up on her hesitancy. "You don't think Lester's guilty, do you?"

"I can't say. And I wouldn't if I could. It's far from settled yet for one thing. For another, I'm not supposed to discuss the trial outside of court."

Louella waved her hands, making her bangle bracelets jingle. "Okay, okay. Forget I mentioned it. Do you know if Estelle's going to be all right?"

"Yes. She has a concussion and they think her ankle may be broken but otherwise she got off easy, considering."

"Thanks to you and the Good Lord." Louella gave her a knowing look. "I did hear about one other thing that happened outside the courthouse. What were you doing with Smith Burnett?"

"What do you mean?" Julie Ann had been combing Louella's damp hair. Now, her hand stilled.

"I understand you two looked pretty cozy. Care to tell me what was going on?"

"Smith was just comforting me after the accident."

"The way I heard it, he was hugging you pretty tight, girl. Do you think that's a good idea?"

"In broad daylight in the middle of town? I can't see a problem," Julie Ann countered. "Besides, there was nothing personal about it. He thought the victim might be me and was relieved to see it wasn't, that's all."

"And why would he think that?"

"It's a long story. I'll fill you in while I set your hair." She pointed at the front of her store and stifled a shiver. "See those holes in the top of my window? That's how it all started."

Smith checked his voice-mail messages, then phoned his office assistant, John, to ask for clarification on one.

"Hey, Smith, good to hear from you," John said. "Are you at the office? Did you see my note about showing the French Town property between four and five o'clock today?"

"That's why I'm calling. Court's adjourned till Monday morning. Do you want me to keep that appointment for you?"

"Would you?" John sounded elated. "That would be great. My son has a soccer match this afternoon and I'd like to watch him play the whole game if I can."

"Sure. No problem," Smith said, frowning as he

glanced at the note in his hand. "I don't recognize this name. Did the guy say where he was from?"

"I don't believe he did. But I know you've been trying to sell the French Town property for months, so I figured it was worth the trip out there to meet with him."

"You're right about that," Smith said. "Anybody who bothers to show up to tour a deserted piece of land and broken-down buildings has to be pretty interested."

"That's what I thought. Besides, it's better if you meet him. He sounded pretty determined that you show him the property, even after I explained that you were tied up in court this week."

Smith's eyebrows arched. "Did he? I suppose he may have talked to me in the past. Where, exactly, were you planning to rendezvous?"

"Next to the WPA marker from the 1940s," John said. "You know. The one that stands at the crossroads, right across from the old wagon repair shop."

"Yeah. Good choice. Can't miss it. Okay. Anything else?"

"Not that I can think of. And thanks for doing this for me, Smith. My son and I both appreciate it."

"No problem. Enjoy the soccer game."

As he hung up, Smith pondered the situation. Four in the afternoon was still broad daylight, so chances were good that this was a genuine prospect. Then again, it never hurt to be careful. He didn't have a pistol close at hand like Julie Ann did, but he had his cell phone. And John knew exactly where he was going so if he had any problems, someone would know where to look.

His imagination added, *Yeah, where to look for the*

body, and he tensed. He wasn't afraid, he was simply cautious. He'd been on hundreds of appointments in the forested hills. This was no different.

But that was before jurors became targets of too many so-called accidents, Smith argued. Instead of disregarding the niggling warning in the back of his mind, he picked up his phone, dialed the sheriff's office and notified Harlan of his plans.

"Better safe than sorry," Smith muttered after he hung up and searched his files for the name on the memo about the French Town property.

To his ultimate chagrin he didn't find any mention of a Harrison, let alone one with the first name of Benjamin. It didn't help Smith's uneasiness that the name was the same as the former U.S. president. He assuaged his concern by arguing that nobody would choose something so obvious as an alias.

By the time he left the office at three-thirty he was feeling a little less uncertain about the whole situation. Still, he harbored enough serious misgivings that he found himself almost reluctant to keep the appointment.

The hair on the back of his neck prickled as he climbed into his SUV and he had to force himself to disregard the instinctive warning. After all, life had to go on. Then again, considering what had happened to poor Estelle Finnerty, efforts to preserve the lives of *all* the jury members had taken on a much greater significance.

Smith knew from experience that no one was guaranteed another breath, another second of life, no matter what their faith—or lack of it. He just wished that circumstances to date hadn't provided so much proof of that incontrovertible fact.

Given what he and Ben had both been through in the Marines, it wasn't at all surprising that they had agreed to share the task of looking after Julie Ann, especially since they had faced peril together overseas. He'd be glad when Ben finally came home, though. This guardian job was proving harder than Smith had thought it would be, especially since he'd realized that his feelings toward the young woman were growing stronger.

Smith's jaw clenched. If she ever guessed that he had started paying more attention to her because of a promise he'd made to Ben, she'd be so mad she might never forgive either of them. That was especially bad because he was now beginning to truly care for her.

Later, as Julie Ann guided her final customer of the afternoon to the dryers, she decided it would be a good time to phone Smith and see how he was doing.

An answering machine at his office took the call. Frustrated, Julie Ann tried his other number, which transferred her to his pager. She finally left a message and waited for him to return her call.

Even after that final customer was gone, Julie Ann was still pacing and waiting. She checked her phone lines to make sure they were in working order, found that they were fine and grew even more upset.

It wasn't at all like Smith to ignore her call, especially since he had professed such strong concern lately. So where was he? Why hadn't he called back?

A tremor zinged through her from her toes to the

nape of her neck. Something was wrong. She had absolutely no reason to think that, yet she was as convinced as if she'd seen Smith in mortal danger.

Fidgeting, she looked at the wall clock, saw how late it was getting, and made a snap decision. She'd close the shop and go see for herself. Walking would be faster than driving, since his office was close by, so she grabbed her purse and headed for the door.

Once she hit the sidewalk, her hurried walk became a jog. Then she was running. Breathless, she got to Serenity Realty and tried the door. It was locked. She shaded her eyes and peered through the windows. The office looked deserted. So where was Smith?

Growing more concerned by the second, Julie Ann scanned the square. Smith's SUV was nowhere in sight. He could have simply gone to show a piece of property but in view of all that had happened to her and to their fellow jurors lately, she wasn't willing to overlook her sense of impending trouble.

The logical thing would be to simply go back to her shop and wait for Smith to return her call. Since the idea of taking no action was totally unacceptable, she did the next best thing. She headed for the sheriff's office.

Bursting through the door she found only Boyd. "Smith Burnett is missing," she announced. When Boyd leaned back in his desk chair and gave her a lazy, good-old-boy grin, she was instantly sorry she had spoken so rashly.

"Naw. He's fine," the gangly deputy said. "Just went on out to French Town to show the old wagoner's place to some city slicker who's got more money than brains."

The strength that had been fueled by her panic left

Julie Ann so rapidly she felt like a deflating balloon. "Are you sure?"

"Positive. He told us where he was headed just in case," Boyd said, still obviously enjoying her temporary loss of composure. "I s'pect he'll be back any minute now."

"How—how long has he been gone?"

"Can't say," Boyd replied. "There was a message on the desk when I got here. Harlan's real bad about not puttin' a date and time on stuff like that. Had to be this afternoon, though, 'cause I was only gone for a few hours."

"I know it was," Julie Ann said, trying to restrain her ire enough to keep from alienating the young deputy. "We were both in court until after lunch."

Boyd sobered. "Yeah. Too bad about Miz Finnerty. I hear she's gonna be okay, though, Lord willin'."

"I'm sure God had a hand in her survival," Julie Ann agreed. *And mine.* "So, when are you or Harlan going to look for Mr. Burnett?"

"All the way out there? Why burn the gas? He'll show up soon. And if he doesn't, it's still up to the sheriff to decide if one of us needs to go take a look-see."

"It'll be getting dark in a few more hours," she reminded him. "Don't you think it would be smarter to go while it's still daylight?"

"Nope." His laconic smile had returned. "I think it'd be smarter not to go off on a wild-goose chase at all."

"Fine." Totally frustrated and unable to think of a snappy retort, she left the sheriff's office and started back toward the beauty salon parking area. If the powers that be weren't going to act, she was.

Suppose Smith got mad at her for worrying about him? Well, too bad. It was all his fault. If he'd returned her calls in a timely manner, she wouldn't need to locate him and see for herself that he was alive and well.

Smith was parked on the side of the dirt road, right next to one of the old stone buildings that had once been part of the business district. The ghost town was located on a main east-west wagon route across northern Arkansas and as such, it had been a perfect place for a repair center. In the days before trucks and cars, a wagon shop with a full-time carpenter and blacksmith was crucial to travelers.

When times had changed, however, the bustling old town had practically dried up and blown away. All that was left were the stone shells of shops and homes, a few rock walls, the carved government marker from the 1940s and enough ticks and chiggers in the tall weeds to repopulate the entire state if need be.

Smith noted the lengthening shadows and checked his watch. It was already well after six. He'd wait another hour or so in case the client was lost on the dirt roads, then head back to Serenity while it was still daylight. This wasn't the first time he'd been stood up, nor would it be the last. That was the real estate business. You did your part and hoped that your client was reliable enough to show up as promised.

The distant sound of a car's motor drew his attention. He scanned the road. There was definitely a cloud of dust being kicked up. It looked as if he was going to get his chance to peddle the derelict property after all.

When the car pulled to a stop parallel to his vehicle, however, he realized he'd been too quick to assume. What was that woman up to now?

Instead of greeting Julie Ann with a smile, he bent down, stuck his head through the passenger-side window and asked firmly, "What are *you* doing out here?"

"Looking for you."

"Why? What's wrong?"

"Nothing. You didn't answer your page and I thought something might be wrong with *you.*"

Smith straightened to peer at the pager clipped to his belt. It was indicating an unread message, as she'd claimed. "Sorry, I didn't notice. Why did you page me?"

She made a face as she climbed out of her car and circled it to stand closer to him. "Beats me. I've been so on edge lately I got worried when I couldn't locate you."

"Since you're out here, would you like to buy a town? I'll make you a great deal."

"No thanks. This place does bring back some fond memories, though. I used to go exploring out here when I was a kid. Grandpa Willis and I came here for target practice, too. He would set up a range for me and I plinked tin cans off the walls till I could hardly hold the gun."

"Your grandfather's been gone for years, hasn't he?"

Julie Ann nodded. "Yes. And I still miss him." She sighed and stared into the distance. "He was my father figure. My own dad wasn't home much and when he was… Let's just say I really needed a loving daddy."

"Everybody does. At least a Heavenly Father."

"Oh, I have Him. Grandma and Grandpa took me to Sunday school every chance they got." Julie Ann shaded her eyes against the late afternoon glare. "So, who are you waiting for?"

"A client named Harrison. I didn't talk to him directly but my assistant did. We're supposed to meet here around five."

"It's a lot later than that."

"I know. I thought you were him when I saw your car coming. I suppose I've been stood up. It happens. At least he picked a nice day to send me off on a wild-goose chase."

"That reminds me. You'd better phone the sheriff's office and tell them you're okay. I just got through chewing Boyd out for not coming to check on your welfare."

Smith flipped open his cell phone, noted that there was no signal and set his jaw. "Can't. There's no service out here. I'll give him a shout when I can pick up a decent signal."

"Okay. I suppose I ought to be going, then."

"You shouldn't have driven way out here in the first place." Realizing how harsh that had sounded, he added, "If you want to stay a while longer and keep me company, I'll treat you to supper."

To his chagrin, she made a face. "Not a good idea. I've already been quizzed about that hug you gave me after Estelle was hit by the truck."

"What hug? Oh, that." He grimaced briefly. "I was just glad that it wasn't you lying in a heap on the street. Guess I got carried away."

"Don't worry," Julie Ann said. "I didn't take it personally and neither should you. I'm not seventeen anymore. You're perfectly safe with me."

He considered saying that he wished she still harbored some affection for him, then stopped himself. Opening up like that would be a big mistake, especially now. Later, after the trial was over, perhaps he'd broach the subject. Then again, before he did that he'd have to confess his promise to her brother, and she might want nothing more to do with him.

Julie Ann sighed as she glanced at the old buildings behind them. "Since I'm already here, I think I'll wander around a little and try to stir up a few good memories."

"I wouldn't do that if I were you. Copperheads and the like will be active now that it's warmed up. You don't want to get a snake bite."

"You're absolutely right. I wish I'd brought my pistol."

"Good thing you didn't," Smith said, wishing he'd come armed, instead. "You might have accidentally shot me."

"That would never happen. Grandpa taught me well."

Smith figured his expression must be overly telling because she took one look at him and started to laugh cynically.

He raised his eyebrows. "What?"

"You're just like all the other macho men in this neck of the woods," she said, shaking her head.

"Me? How?"

"Because you think that being armed should be totally a male privilege. Well, get over it, mister. This woman is as capable of handling a gun as any good old boy. Maybe more so. I'll be glad to prove it to you the first chance I get."

He would have disagreed with her if he could have come up with a plausible counterargument. The trouble was, he believed her. Totally. And considering they were out in the middle of nowhere, alone, he almost wished she had brought her gun along.

If he hadn't been so eager to keep this appointment he might have stopped at home to pick up one of his own pistols, even though he had never applied for a "concealed carry" permit. That would have been the most sensible thing to do, especially in view of all that had happened in the past few weeks.

Smith scanned the deserted buildings. This terrain was more hilly and a lot greener than the foreign territories where he'd faced armed enemies, but its forbidding atmosphere was all too similar to suit him. There were too many places to hide. Too many deepening afternoon shadows. Too many unknowns.

"I don't want you wandering off. Stay here with me," he said, realizing immediately that he had just guaranteed her defiance.

When she said, "Oh, yeah?" Smith gritted his teeth. He knew there would be no stopping her now.

SEVEN

The beauty of the balmy, spring evening in the Ozarks would normally have warmed Julie Ann's heart. Not today. Today, she was so on edge she was furious. Someone had done this to her; had stolen her peace and left her jumping at shadows. It wasn't fair. It also wasn't going to keep her from doing as she wished. Neither was Smith Burnett.

Watching where she stepped, she cautiously threaded her way between the broken-down exterior walls of the old buildings. Most fell below her waist due to the rigors of Arkansas winters and the ease of gathering the stones from the old town in lieu of collecting them in the wild. Many a newer chimney or wall had been built from the wreckage. Julie Ann didn't blame those who had helped themselves to the ready-made construction material. It was just sad to see a place with so many memories literally disappearing.

Growing more relaxed by the minute, she paused next to an old wall rife with lush vines and the red, belled blossoms of a wild trumpet creeper. The native plants best survived neglect, she noted, so much so that many of them were all that seemed to support some of the shaky walls.

Suddenly, Julie Ann's skin prickled. She tensed, not knowing why. An instant later there was a loud, sharp crack of sound followed by an explosion of the rock beneath the vines just above her head.

She ducked instinctively. "What in the world...?"

The characteristics of the echoing, zinging sound registered a split second later. It was a gunshot! And not a little .22 this time, either. Somebody was shooting a high-powered rifle—at her!

Crouching lower, she heard a second shot reverberate. Another chunk of rock shattered and rained tiny pebbles and dust over her.

The marksman was zeroing in. That last bullet landed right where her head would have been if she hadn't hunkered down.

Ignoring the insect-infested underbrush she'd been so careful to avoid, she started to move. Bent low, she darted around the nearest wall, taking care to keep it between her and the direction where the sound of the shots had apparently originated.

What now? Should she stay put or try to get back to her car? Suppose the assailant didn't know Smith was here, too? If she led the shooter away first, she could then double back and safely rejoin Smith.

That idea would have been perfect if she had not looked up and seen him racing toward her, head down, zigzagging like a combat veteran in the midst of an attack or a football player dodging members of the opposing team.

"I'm okay!" Julie Ann shouted.

Smith skidded to a stop, cupped his hands around his mouth and yelled, "Where are you?"

Before Julie Ann had time to take a breath to answer, another sharp crack resounded across the open space.

To her horror, Smith Burnett rose up, spun to his left and dropped like a rock.

There was a heaviness about his shoulder and a dull ache in his arm. Smith realized he was lying on the ground and began to sit up before he fully realized what must have happened to him.

Julie Ann. He had to get to Julie Ann.

Only something was very wrong. Incredulous, he stared at his upper arm. He had grabbed it instinctively, holding it tightly while blood seeped between his fingers. He had been *shot*. Three tours of duty overseas without a scratch and he'd been wounded a few miles from home. What irony.

The urge to curse was great. Instead, he crawled awkwardly behind a wall and sent up a quick prayer of thanks that his arm had been hit instead of some more vital area.

He tensed, waiting for a further attack. There was total silence. Birds had stopped singing. Insects no longer chirped.

Someone called his name from afar. "Smith!"

"Stay put," he shouted back. "I'll come to you."

When Julie Ann replied, "In a pig's eye," Smith realized that her voice now sounded much closer.

A moment later she vaulted over the low wall and

landed in a crouch beside him. Unshed tears immediately filled her eyes. "Oh, Smith! I thought you said you were fine."

"I exaggerated, but I'm okay. Keep your head down. Did you see who was doing the shooting?"

"No." She gently touched his shoulder with a trembling hand. "I was admiring some wildflowers when somebody put the first shot into the wall right above me."

"Careless hunters?"

"Right. And you and I look like Bambi?"

"I get your point." He grimaced, hoping she hadn't noticed. "We can't stay here. We don't dare show ourselves, either."

"Don't worry. He's gone," Julie Ann said.

"How do you know?"

"Well, for starters, I had to be partially in the open when I ran back to you and nobody shot at me then."

"You *what?*"

"Simmer down, mister. I dodged and ducked just like you did. Besides, now that I've thought about it, I doubt the guy was after me in the first place."

"Why?"

"Because you were lured out here alone. No one else was supposed to be anywhere around."

"You're right. Not that that makes my arm feel much better." He raised himself into a full sitting position and prepared to stand.

Julie Ann jumped up and held out her hand. "Here. I'll help you."

"I can manage." He squelched a groan of pain as he

got to his feet. "Just keep your eyes open and stay behind me so you don't make yourself a target again."

"I told you…"

"I know what you *told* me," Smith said flatly, his jaw muscles clenching as they started back toward their cars. "But that doesn't mean whoever shot me won't figure two-for-the-price-of-one is even better."

"When you're right, you're right. I just wish you weren't."

Smith nodded soberly. "Yeah. So do I."

Julie Ann knew he had to be in terrible pain and it hurt her to imagine it. The question was, would he swallow his pride long enough to allow her to chauffeur him back to town? Rather than ask, she simply hurried ahead to grab her purse from her car, then jumped into his SUV and slid behind the wheel.

She was prepared to argue but he fooled her by getting in on the passenger side and slamming the door with his good hand.

"Fulton County Hospital?" she asked, relieved to note that Smith had left his keys in the ignition.

"Yeah." He slid down in the seat and added, "Get us out of here before our friend puts us in his crosshairs again."

That sounded fine to Julie Ann. Her whole body had begun trembling when she'd seen Smith injured but she wasn't about to let any weakness show. Not when he needed her.

Once they got back to town and she delivered him to the hospital, however, she was going to give her turbulent emotions free rein. She was hurt to the quick seeing him on the ground, bleeding. Even now, just thinking about it made her stomach churn and her hands shake.

She gripped the wheel more tightly and accelerated out of the turns as smoothly as she could. The larger vehicle was much more powerful and more stable on the rocky dirt track than her little car would have been, which made her thankful she had chosen to drive the SUV. It hadn't been a conscious decision. It had nevertheless been the right one.

Briefly glancing in the rearview mirror, she saw no sign of a pursuer. "Looks like we got away."

"I'll believe that when we're safely back in Serenity," Smith said. "Keep your eyes open. Don't get too complacent."

"You were just *shot*. Do you really think I could be complacent?"

"Okay, okay. You're right." He grimaced. "I'm not thinking too clearly right now."

"And I shouldn't have snapped at you. Sorry."

As they rounded the corner where the French Town Road met the Y of the dirt track leading to the town of Camp, she was startled to encounter an oncoming car. It was not only taking up the center of the roadway, it didn't give ground.

Whipping the SUV hard to the right, she almost overcorrected and careened off into the drainage ditch along the berm.

Smith braced himself. "Look out!"

"I see him." Her maneuver had been barely enough

to skirt the black, Humvee-like vehicle in the first place. When it swerved into her path once again she was flabbergasted.

Time seemed to crawl by. Seconds felt like hours. Realizing that the other driver was not the innocent party she had first assumed, she waited till the last possible moment, then jerked the wheel hard in the opposite direction, managing to squeeze by on its right.

"What an idiot. He's crazy," Julie Ann screeched.

Smith had slewed in the seat and was looking back. "Uh-oh. Floor it. He's turning around."

"What?" She peered into the side mirrors and gasped. Smith was right. Dust behind them was thick, yet she could see that the black car was sliding into a U-turn. It was clearly going to pursue them.

"How fast will this thing go?" she asked, pushing the accelerator to the floor.

"I think we're about to find out."

Every muscle in her body was taut. Her teeth clenched. She gave a barely perceptible nod. "You've got that right. Hang on. This could get real bumpy."

Julie Ann kept telling herself she could outdrive whoever was on their tail. The adrenaline coursing through her affirmed that conclusion. This was no time for self-doubt or indecisiveness.

The windows of the Humvee vehicle were heavily tinted, making it impossible to see inside as it had passed, so she had no idea how many men were in pursuit. At this point it hardly mattered, since she and Smith weren't armed and the others probably were.

"Probably, nothing," she muttered, disgusted with

herself for leaving her gun at home. "What'll we do if they catch us?"

When Smith didn't answer, a quick glance in his direction told her that his injury was being aggravated by their wild ride. Though he hadn't released his hold on his upper arm, more blood was flowing. That was not a good sign.

She opened her mouth to ask him if he was all right, then closed it without speaking. Of course he wasn't all right. Neither of them were. Smith had been wounded and she was likely to wreck them both with her race-car-type driving.

Well, she had no choice. It was run or be caught. That last notion did not appeal to her one bit.

Thoughts jumbled, head spinning, Julie Ann reached out to God. No adequate prayer came to mind so she merely shouted a silent call for help.

The SUV splashed through a concrete-paved swale, spraying the standing creek water on both sides like the wake of a speedboat. That gave her an idea. There was a remote possibility that she could ditch their pursuers if she pretended to turn onto Heart Road going toward Saddle, then took the unmarked bypass in use since that old, narrow bridge had washed out months before. If the guys in the Humvee car kept going…

Her eyes widened. The heavens hadn't opened up and miraculously shown her the way, but she didn't need that kind of vivid convincing. This was the answer to her wordless, inadequate prayer. She knew it as surely as she knew her own name, which would be "mud" if she didn't pull off the misdirection.

"Hang on," she shouted to Smith. "I'm going up the road to Saddle."

"That bridge is out," he yelled back.

"Everybody in Serenity knows that. Hopefully, the guys behind us aren't from around here."

The side trail was little more than a suggestion of a real road. Overgrown and narrow, it was barely wide enough for one vehicle at a time to pass and could easily be mistaken for a private driveway.

Julie Ann turned that corner so fast she feared the SUV might roll. It teetered, then fell back onto all four wheels and straightened out just in time.

There was no way to tell if the Humvee vehicle had followed without slowing to look back. She wasn't about to do that. Sticking to the center of the narrow trail she continued as fast as she dared without hitting the trees that lined the sides.

Overhanging branches slapped the windshield. Vines whipped past, grabbing at them. In a few more seconds they would connect with the safe side of the damaged bridge and know if her plan had worked.

Smith was leaning forward, peering ahead, as they emerged from the side road. "You did it!" he shouted. "I don't believe it."

In spite of their precarious situation, Julie Ann smiled. There sat the black Humvee auto, nose down in the creek, rear wheels hanging from what was left of the washed-out bridge. "Praise the Lord the county road crew didn't get around to repairing that yet," she yelled, ecstatic.

"Don't slow down," Smith warned. "They're getting

out. And they look madder than a wet hen. I think one of them has a rifle."

"Probably the one he used earlier," she answered. "If you have a signal on your phone now, how about trying to call the sheriff?"

Smith looked at his phone. "It's showing a low signal."

Still, he tried it and Julie was thrilled when the call went through.

She didn't resume normal speed until they were almost to the hospital. Although they were now in the clear, Smith kept grumbling. "I never should have gone out there alone. I *knew* better."

"You weren't alone," Julie Ann reminded him. "I was with you. And since we've finally ditched our tail, it looks to me as though the Good Lord was with us both."

Had he felt better he might have also mentioned that she'd gone looking for him because of an unexplained feeling of foreboding. Since she didn't think he'd care to hear her prattling on about that, or about anything else right now, she kept silent. Later, however, she fully intended to tell him why she had ventured into the countryside in search of him.

It had not been a logical choice. Nor had her actions been well thought out. They had simply been as necessary as breathing. She had had to find Smith. To know he was all right. Because he was so important to her.

Suppose she had not heeded her instincts? What then?

Julie Ann shivered as the alternative scenario played

out in her mind. If she had not been there when Smith had been hurt, he might have had trouble getting himself back to town, not to mention outdriving whoever was after them.

Worse, she added, blanching, the man who had shot him could have approached while he was down and finished him off without worrying about being observed. Just like that, Smith would have been gone forever.

The unacceptable concept brought unshed tears and made her heart pound. What was happening to her quaint, safe little town? Where was the peace? The tranquility? The serenity of Serenity?

Where, indeed. It certainly wasn't evident anymore.

EIGHT

Smith climbed out of the car as soon as Julie Ann parked near the emergency room. Even though he had alerted the sheriff and told him where to look for their assailants, he kept watching the street for any sign of the Humvee vehicle as they walked inside together.

When they found no one in the reception area, he loudly announced, "Hey! Anybody home? I've been shot."

His cry brought a scrubs-clad nurse. She ushered him into an exam room, placed him on the padded table with a cursory glance at his injury and then left to summon a doctor.

Julie Ann stood close and gently caressed his uninjured shoulder. "How're you doing now?"

"Fine. Thanks to you. If you ever need another job, I'll give you references for driving an ambulance. Or a getaway car."

He was pleased to see that his quip brought a slight smile to her lovely face. She really did look beautiful at that moment. Thoughts of what he would have done, how he might have survived if she had not been with him, were not reassuring and he wanted her to know exactly how he felt.

"You probably saved my life," he told her, sobering. "I owe you one."

Julie Ann's smile grew. "Maybe *more* than one, if you stop to think about it. But don't worry about that right now." Her lips trembled slightly as she glanced at his shoulder. "That looks pretty nasty."

"It's messy but not deep."

"Well, don't show me, okay? I'm not feeling all that steady on my feet." She sighed deeply, tellingly. "You had me pretty scared."

"You and me both." Smith would have taken her hand if his hadn't been covered with blood. "I wasn't exaggerating about how beholden I am to you."

He wanted to say more, and might have, if the middle-aged doctor had not bustled into the exam room accompanied by two nurses. Seeing the other man's raised eyebrows and the way he glanced at Julie Ann with undisguised suspicion, Smith was quick to explain.

"Don't look at her, doc. She didn't shoot me. And we have no idea who did."

Although the medical staff didn't comment directly, Smith could tell that they weren't fully accepting his account. He didn't blame them. It did sound pretty lame. If he hadn't known about the other recent attacks and close calls, he'd have been skeptical, too.

He was just thankful that *he* was doing the bleeding, not Julie Ann.

By the time X rays had been taken and the wound bandaged, the sheriff had arrived to take the required report.

"I'm gettin' a tad sick of you folks here," Harlan said. "That car you told me to look for in the creek was long gone by the time Boyd got there." He eyed the bandage. "What brought all this on?"

"I was out on a call to show property in French Town like I'd told you. Remember?" Smith replied. "As you can see, somebody shot me." He saw Harlan pause to consider Julie Ann's presence so he added, "And, no, we didn't see anybody. We didn't even see where the shots came from. Since we were chased and nearly forced off the road, I'm pretty sure that black Humvee had plenty to do with it."

"Miz Jones was there?" Harlan asked, making notes.

"Yes. She followed to check on me after Boyd wouldn't take her concerns seriously."

The portly sheriff made a dour face. "He told me she'd been by the office. Didn't say she was going to go lookin' for you on her own, though."

"Good thing for me that she did," Smith said, sitting up while the nurse adjusted a blue canvas sling to cradle his bandaged arm. "We'll need to go back out there and pick up her car. She drove me to the hospital in mine."

"Boyd and me'll fetch it for her," Harlan said. "That's the least we can do. You gonna be able to get yourself home okay?"

Julie Ann spoke up. "I'll take care of him. You just find out who shot at us. Again."

That brought a deepening scowl to the lawman's round face. "You were shot at, too?"

"Yes. Twice. Only I ducked and Smith didn't."

"Smart girl. Too bad you didn't have something with

you to shoot back. If I remember right, old Willis taught you plenty about guns."

"Maybe I will the next time," she said flatly.

Harlan raised his eyebrows but instead of commenting to her he spoke to Smith. "You've got military training so you won't have to take the regular class for me to issue you a temporary permit to carry a concealed weapon. When you're up to it, stop by the office and we'll do the paperwork if that's what you want." He held out the clipboard. "Just read what I wrote, sign at the bottom and I'll be on my way."

"Okay. What now, Sheriff?" Smith asked, doing as instructed and hoping that changing the subject would keep Julie Ann from demanding the same kind of legal permit.

"I'll take a look-see around the old town when we pick up Miz Julie Ann's car. Don't 'spect we'll find much, though. It's a pretty big place." He touched the brim of his hat in parting. "Y'all take care, y'hear?"

Smith slid off the end of the table so he was standing next to Julie Ann, then paused momentarily. "It looks as though I can walk."

She took his good arm. "Just the same, I'm going to make sure you get home safely." When Smith smiled, she peered into his eyes and added, "No argument? You must be in shock."

"Nope," he said, grinning. "I just know when I'm well-off. I am kind of a mess to be taking you out to dinner the way I had offered. We can have a pizza delivered to my place."

"I turned you down, remember? Besides, there's no pizza delivery in Serenity."

"There is if you have a buddy who lives practically

next door to Hickory Station. After we get to my house, I'll call Logan Malloy and ask him to stop by—and bring us food."

"Brother Logan is my pastor," Julie Ann said, sounding surprised.

"Well, well, what a small world. I sold him that house he and Becky live in. He's been after me to come to his church ever since. Maybe I'll have to reconsider."

"I'd like that," she said. "Besides, if I'm going to spend much time at your house I'll need a chaperone."

Smith chuckled in spite of the thumps of pain in his arm every time his heart pulsed. "A chaperone? Do you think I'm dangerous?"

"No. But I've already told you we were the subject of rumors after that incident in the square. The last thing I need is to have people imagining that I'm a loose woman."

Her honesty and obvious embarrassment made Smith laugh softly before he said, "Anybody who thinks that of you is not paying attention."

"Flattery will get you nowhere, Mr. Burnett."

He laughed again, louder this time. "As long as it gets me to the pharmacy for some pain pills and then home, I'll be satisfied. Come on. You can drive."

"As if I'd let you try it in your condition."

"That's what I'd figured," Smith said. "And I've learned the hard way that it's not a good idea to argue with you or tell you that you *can't* do anything."

Julie Ann laughed. "I knew you were a smart man."

Smith waited in the car while Julie Ann dashed into the pharmacy to pick up his prescription. When she returned and handed him the white paper sack containing his medication, he was grinning from ear to ear.

"You look mighty pleased with yourself. If I didn't know better I'd think you'd already had one of those pain pills," she said, immensely relieved to see that he seemed to have improved.

"Nope. I'm just high on life. I guess survival will do that to a guy. And you don't have to worry about not having a chaperone. I called Logan while you were in the drugstore. He's going to meet us at my house in a few minutes."

"Thanks. It's not that I don't trust you, personally, it's just…" She didn't have to finish that thought to see from Smith's expression that he understood.

"I know. I grew up here just like you did. I know how the grapevine works. One person stubs a toe and half a dozen folks end up limping."

"Exactly." She slid behind the wheel and started the car. "I'd heard you bought the old Crowder place. Are you living out there?"

"I am now. It needed a lot of work but we finally got it renovated. Which reminds me about French Town. Harlan never asked us where we were standing when we were shot at. Didn't you think that was a bit strange?"

She shrugged. "Not really. There's no way we could have described the exact spots, even if we'd had a map right in front of us."

"I guess you're right. My imagination seems to be on overload at the moment."

He isn't the only one, she thought, biting her lower

lip. Whoever had set up Smith at the old town site had apparently known him well enough to predict that he'd respond eagerly to a chance to sell that particular piece of property. They'd also have known that court had not reconvened after Estelle's accident. Therefore, somebody sinister was closely involved in the daily life of Serenity.

Somebody she probably knew.

Somebody who was a cold-blooded killer.

She tried to stifle a shiver but Smith saw her shake. "Are you all right?" he asked.

"I'd be better if I didn't feel like the duck decoy in a carnival shooting gallery. We can't keep dodging forever, you know. One of these days it's going to catch up with us and be worse than it has been so far. If not for you or me, then for another juror."

"So, you do believe it's all connected."

"How can I not think so, given everything that's happened?" She gave him a quick look of deeply felt concern. "I'm so, so thankful you're going to be all right."

"Thank you, Julie Ann. I'm just beginning to realize how close you came to being seriously injured, too. We've got to tell the judge what's happened if Harlan doesn't do it for us."

"All right. Do you think they'll declare a mistrial?" She hated to imagine another panel of jurors going through the same rigors they had, but she didn't see what other options there might be.

"I don't know. Just because something seems sensible to us doesn't mean that's how it's supposed to be handled according to law. Besides, we don't know if our problems have anything to do with Lester's trial and if Harlan doesn't catch whoever is doing this, we may never find out for sure."

"That's what worries me. When we talk to Brother Logan, I want to get his advice."

"I hardly think this is a situation that requires pastoral counseling."

"Neither do I," Julie Ann said. "Logan Malloy used to be a private detective. I think he may be able to advise us on further steps to take."

"For instance?"

She knew she must look self-satisfied and perhaps just a little overconfident but nevertheless she continued. "I don't know about you, in view of your injury, but I intend to go back to French Town tomorrow or the next day and have a look around myself."

When his jaw dropped and he gasped incredulously, it struck her so funny that she grinned. "Don't worry. I'll take my gun."

She burst out laughing when he replied, "That's what I was afraid of."

Logan Malloy did not come to Smith's house alone. By the time Julie Ann wheeled into his driveway, the pastor and his wife, Becky, were both waiting.

Becky ran to Julie Ann and gave her a sisterly hug. "Oh, honey, we heard about the shooting. What a terrible thing. Are you all right?"

"I'm a lot better than Smith is," she said, circling the SUV to join him and Logan.

"She's right about that." Smith led the way toward his

covered front porch. "Let's go inside so I can put on a clean shirt and get washed up. Then I'll tell you everything."

He hadn't intended to conduct a strategy meeting but since that was how it was turning out, he invited everyone to gather around the dining room table, share his pizza and listen to the whole story. He'd known little about Logan's past other than he had not always been a pastor. Now that they had discussed the events surrounding the shooting, however, Smith was amazed at the other man's calm expertise.

When Logan concluded his opinion by saying, "I think you should both back off and let the sheriff handle it," Smith could see that Julie Ann was far from convinced.

"I don't think Ms. Jones is in agreement," Smith remarked, smiling at her to soften his criticism. "She's already told me she intends to investigate on her own."

Logan frowned. "That would be very unsafe and also unwise. The judge determines what evidence is shown to the jury, and if there is a connection, any efforts on your part could disqualify you and ruin everything."

Smith thought the pastor's words might have had the desired effect until Logan's wife, Becky, chimed in with, "Oh, hush. That was the same thing you told me when I was having problems with Aunt Effie and that all turned out okay."

Her husband gave her a sobering look. "Only because Effie wasn't really a criminal and your father wasn't out to get you, Becky. This situation is totally different. Julie Ann and Smith are facing real bullets and it seems to me that staying out of it as much as possible is the only sensible course of action."

"Out of it?" Julie Ann sounded irate. "How much can we stay out of anything when trouble is chasing us all over the Ozarks? Smith didn't tell you about the bullet holes in the window of my shop or how my tires were flattened. And all that happened first."

Logan steepled his fingers, looking thoughtful before he said, "All right. Tell you what I'll do. I personally think Harlan is straight. Just in case, however, I'll have some of my old friends in law enforcement look into the justice system here. I may not be able to share that information with you, but I will be able to better advise you."

Julie Ann eyed Smith. "Do you really think he'll be able to stay on the jury? I mean, what about his injury?"

"I can serve with my arm in a sling," Smith said. "As long as I'm not taking the pain pills I don't think it will disqualify me." He could see doubt in Julie's pretty hazel gaze but he figured as long as the judge and attorneys didn't object, he'd continue to show up in court. If he had to drop out, who would look after Julie Ann? He had to be there, no matter what. If he was bumped off the actual jury, he'd station himself with the other onlookers and keep watch from there.

Everyone had to pass through a metal detector to get into the courtroom so there was little chance of actual danger to her while she was in the jury box. When she left, however, that changed. And he would be there then, too. As long as he had breath left in his body, he'd keep her safe.

NINE

In the end, Julie Ann allowed Logan and Becky to drive her home. She hid her nervousness pretty well as she chatted with Becky in the well-lit front room of the farmhouse while Logan checked the rest of the rooms for intruders.

He ultimately pronounced the house safe and headed for the door with his wife. "Everything looks secure enough," he said. "Just see that you keep the doors and windows locked and trust Andy's instincts. I can't imagine anyone getting past a dog like that."

"Neither can I."

Julie Ann stood at the open front door and watched her friends get into their car. That was another special blessing of life in a place like Serenity. Even if the Malloys had not been her pastor and his wife, they would have made just as much effort to help her. Country people did thoughtful things like that.

When their car's taillights disappeared in the distance, she was suddenly struck by a wave of irrational fear. Slamming the front door she made doubly certain it was locked. The only thing that gave her pause was

realizing that she was virtually stranded there until
Harlan and Boyd returned her car. If something else bad
happened, her only recourse would be her regular telephone because she'd left her cell on the seat of her car.
What if someone disconnected her land line to keep her
from calling for help?

Near panic, she lifted the receiver and listened for a
dial tone. Hearing its comforting drone she was satisfied.
Her connection to the rest of world was in order. She had
nothing to worry about. So why was she still trembling
as if she'd just witnessed Smith being shot all over again?

That heart-wrenching picture would always be with
her, she knew. It would haunt her waking hours as well
as her nightmares. There had been times, when he'd
been fighting overseas, that she'd dreamed of him being
wounded. Even those vivid images had been nothing
compared to reality. She'd thought her heart would stop
when he'd fallen.

But he had survived. He could have been taken from
her forever and he'd survived. Praise the Lord!

At that moment she was so thankful, so overcome
with gratitude to her Heavenly Father, she wanted to
raise her hands and shout for joy. If Smith had been
within reach, she might have hugged and kissed him re-
gardless of their rocky history.

A sudden urge to hear his voice washed over her.
She reached for the phone and dialed. Just as the connection was being completed she changed her mind
and hung up. It was silly to bother him. After all, he
was probably already asleep and he needed plenty of
rest in order to recover.

She plopped into her recliner and leaned it back before reaching for the remote control to turn on the TV. Her left hand groped the carpet beside the chair. Where had that remote gotten to? She was sure she'd left it right where she always did but a cursory search failed to produce it. How odd. Maybe Bubbles had decided it would make a good chew toy and had carried it off.

Weariness kept her from continuing to look. Who cared if the TV was off? Not her. All she really needed was a nap, preferably one that lasted all evening and all night, too.

Although she knew she should shower and get ready for bed, she didn't want to leave the living room or switch off any lights and have to deal with the darkness. Worn to a frazzle, she decided to stay right where she was and merely close her eyes for a few minutes.

She barely heard Andy when he lay beside her chair. Sleep edged at her consciousness. Though her mind was far from keen, she still recited a brief prayer, ending with "And, Father, thank You for Smith's and my deliverance today. Please continue to protect us and our fellow jurors. I ask this in Jesus' name. Amen."

Hugging herself, she pictured Smith and lovingly whispered one more thing. "Good night. God bless you."

Smith had taken one pain pill and slept for several hours on his sofa before waking due to mounting discomfort.

As he lay there, staring at the moonlight reflected on the high, concave ceiling of his sitting room, he thought about Julie Ann and how brave she had been, how well she had conducted herself in the midst of a potentially lethal situation.

Closing his eyes, he pictured her leaning over him, braced to sprint for cover like a commando and standing guard as if she thought she could hold off any threat empty-handed. She was truly a wonder. Women like her had been among the stalwart pioneers who had crossed the Rockies in covered wagons. He could easily imagine her, dressed in a calico sunbonnet, with that old holster of her grandfather's strapped on at the waist of her long skirt.

As he rolled to one side, swung his legs over the edge of the sofa and sat up, he glanced at his answering machine. The red light was blinking. He hadn't heard the phone ring. Maybe the pain medicine had worked better than he'd thought.

He reached over and pushed the play button. There was no recorded message, although the digital readout showed that the caller had been local. Funny. He didn't recognize that number.

Not overly concerned, he decided to get a glass of water, take his next course of medication and wait till morning before bothering to see who the unknown number belonged to. After all, it was the middle of the night. No one would expect him to call back now.

Returning with the water and getting out a dose of pain meds, he paused with the pill in his hand. That phone number. Should he know it? His brow furrowed. It wasn't his assistant's and it wasn't Julie Ann's shop, either. Could it be her home?

A tightening in his gut warned that it might be. She might need him.

"And what if she does?" Smith asked himself, staring at the medication in his palm. "I can't do anything about it if I take this."

Okay. He could delay taking a painkiller for a while and tough it out. That still didn't mean the number was Julie Ann's. What if it wasn't? Or, more importantly, what if the answering machine had merely been the catalyst for his concern and she'd come to mind because she truly *did* need him?

That notion brought chills that raced through him like slivers of iced lightning. He closed his eyes for a moment and reached out with his mind to the God he had long neglected.

Smith hadn't prayed since he'd left the Marines, yet he had no trouble doing so for Julie Ann's benefit. All he needed was some sign that she was in jeopardy and he'd gladly act, whatever it took.

His sense of urgency and peril increased till he realized he was sweating. Either that or he'd developed the fever that often accompanied a gunshot wound, he concluded, remembering what the medics in the field had always warned against.

The way Smith saw it, there was only one thing to do. He had to look up Julie Ann's home number. In a small community like Serenity it couldn't be that hard to find, even if her last name was practically generic.

Julie Ann awoke with a start, temporarily disoriented. Andy still lay beside her chair, dozing peacefully, so what had brought her out of such a sound sleep? Had she been having a nightmare? She didn't think so.

Blinking to adjust to the dimness of the room, she listened. A soft, mewling sound was coming from the direction of the front porch.

Her first thought was that someone had dumped another homeless kitten. That kind of thing was always occurring. City folks assumed that any pet could fend for itself if it was left far enough out in the country. They never thought about the fact that a tiny domestic animal was more likely to become a coyote's dinner than it was to catch enough mice to survive, let alone thrive.

The strength and direction of the sound remained constant. Julie Ann laid her hand atop Andy's head to rouse him and saw him immediately prick his ears and incline his head. "You hear it, too, don't you, boy? I'm glad. I was beginning to think I was imagining things."

Andy stretched, then rose and looked at her quizzically.

"What do you think it is, huh? Do we have another orphan to adopt?"

His tail wagged. He licked her hand.

Rising, Julie Ann strapped on her grandfather's pistol but left it in the holster. "Okay. I'll go look as long as you come along."

The big dog padded smoothly to the door and stood there with his tail flagging, his eyes bright, his ears erect.

Julie Ann flipped on the porch light and reached for the lock, then paused. Listened. Considered. If it had been dangerous to open the door, surely Andy would have barked the way he always did.

Crouching next to the dog, Julie Ann pressed her ear against the door. That was the fussing noise of a baby all right, only it wasn't a kitten. It was human.

"Who in the world…?"

She was about to jerk open the door when it occurred to her that her house was a very unlikely place for someone to abandon a child, let alone a baby. Still…

"Father, what should I do?" she prayed aloud. "If it's a real baby it must be freezing out there."

And if it isn't real?

If it wasn't, and she opened the door, there was no telling what danger might be lurking.

Her trembling hand reached toward the lock just as her telephone began to ring.

By now, Smith was positive he was phoning Julie Ann. There had been several semi-anonymous J. Joneses listed. This particular number matched the one on his answering machine. It *had* to be hers.

When she said, "Hello," his relief was quickly replaced by concern when he heard the apprehension in her voice.

"Are you all right?" he asked without bothering to identify himself.

"Smith? Is that you? What's wrong?"

"I asked you first."

"Nothing, except…"

His hand tightened on the receiver. "Except what? Do you have another prowler?"

"I—I don't think so. I just heard a funny noise on the porch. It sounds like a baby crying. I can't just leave a helpless baby outside all night."

"Then call Harlan and let him check. It's his job, remember?"

"He'll be sure I'm crazy if there's nothing out there."

Smith was flustered beyond belief. That woman had a ready excuse for everything. "Shall I call him for you?"

"No. Don't even consider it."

"You don't intend to phone him, do you?" Waiting for her reply, Smith became even more convinced that she was once again planning to take matters into her own hands. As far as he could see, there was only one remaining course of action and it was his to carry out.

"Julie Ann," he said firmly. "Listen to me. The noise you heard may very well be a trap. It's a common ruse. Enemy combatants used to do that kind of thing all the time, then set off bombs when our troops were fool enough to fall for it because we were worried about civilians. Trust me. You do *not* want to go outside."

"What if it's not a fake?"

"If the sound was a real baby, it won't hurt the infant to wait a few more minutes until I can get there."

"You can't drive. You're wounded."

He took a deep breath and prayed she'd listen to him without prejudging. "Look. I know you think you can handle anything that comes along all by yourself—and you probably can under normal circumstances. I'm not criticizing your capabilities. I'm telling you that I'm coming over. If you choose to wait for me, fine. If you decide to open the door and look before I get there, I can't stop you."

"But you'll be mad. Is that what you're saying?"

"I'll be furious."

"I think I get the idea."

"Good, because I don't want to show up and find your dead body on your porch." He hated to be so blunt but he was willing to do or say anything if it would protect her from irrational bravado.

"Okay, okay. Are you sure you're well enough to drive?"

All Smith said was "Yes" before he slammed down the receiver.

Because the problem of undressing for bed had been too difficult, he had slept in his clothes. Now, he was glad. If he hadn't been dressed already it would have taken him a lot longer to grab his Colt .45 and his keys and hurry to the SUV.

As far as Smith was concerned, only one thing was vital. Getting to Julie Ann. Immediately.

Julie Ann sat there, staring at the now-silent telephone and muttering to herself. "What possessed Smith to phone? It didn't make any sense for him to call at all, let alone at precisely the right moment to stop me from opening the door."

She supposed, if she stretched her imagination, it was possible to see the Lord's hand behind such perfect timing. It was also possible that Smith's decision had been a coincidence.

Smiling, she thought of the combined alternative her friends sometimes suggested, a "God-incidence." Either way, she was glad it had happened.

The sound of a baby on her porch had not stopped,

nor had it changed since it began, leading her to conclude that Smith may have been right. She didn't have much experience with little children but she figured a real baby would have varied its cries, especially since they had been going on for several minutes.

Peering between the slats of the blinds covering her front windows, she watched the road and waited for Smith's headlights to appear. The longer she stood there, the more she worried about him.

"That man is exasperating," she told Andy, who remained at her side. "Imagine. Driving in his condition. He's crazy." And dear. And sweet. And all the other appealing traits she had often thought of but dared not voice. Above all, she was afraid of him suspecting she was once again falling for him. Surely, she could appreciate his finer attributes without fawning all over him like a lovesick adolescent.

"Can I?" she asked herself. "Oh, sure. All I have to do is keep hanging around that insufferable man until the trial is over. By then, I'll probably be so crazy about him I won't know up from down. I hardly do, now."

With a sigh she dropped the blinds back into place and began to pace the small living room. Frustration was far too mild a word to describe her mental state and she had no idea how she was going to keep her cool long enough to cope with another visit from Smith Burnett.

Truth to tell, she was almost as apprehensive about that as she was about opening her front door.

TEN

Smith was having difficulty steering with his sore left arm still in the sling. He covered the final quarter mile to the old farm, but he didn't see anyone or anything moving on the porch as he approached. Considering all that had happened recently, there was no telling what was actually going on.

No cars were visible, other than his own, as he parked in front of the isolated house. Julie Ann's car wasn't there either, indicating that Harlan had not yet brought it back from French Town.

Smith turned off the ignition, grabbed the .45, climbed out of the SUV and scaled her front steps two at a time, ignoring the pain that the jarring pace caused his injury.

Julie Ann jerked open the door before he had time to knock. She didn't appear very pleased. "That was way fast. You must have driven like a maniac."

"Only because I was worried about you."

She peered past him. "I don't see any baby, do you?"

"No. Did you see anybody else out here?"

"No."

"Well, it obviously wasn't a real baby on your doorstep because there's no sign of it now. Maybe you were dreaming."

Her lips pressed into a thin line as she shook her head. "No way. Andy heard it, too. The funny thing is, he didn't start to bark or act interested until we heard your car coming."

Stepping back, Smith kept his automatic pistol aimed into the dark distance as he began to scan the porch. A small, shadowy object lay beneath one of the metal garden chairs on her porch. "What's that?"

Julie Ann stuck her head out, said, "Beats me," then edged past Smith to investigate. She retrieved the black, plastic, rectangular object and showed it to him.

"It's a tape recorder," he said, scowling.

"You're right. And it's not mine. Do you think it was supposed to be a trap like the ones you told me about?"

She pushed the rewind button, then Play.

Smith thought she was going to drop the tape recorder when it began to emit sounds that mimicked a softly crying infant. "Was that what you heard?"

Blanching, she nodded. "Yes. It's so faint that if I hadn't misplaced my TV remote I probably wouldn't have been able to hear it over the program noise." Her shoulders sagged as she placed the machine on the chair. "And now that I've touched that thing, I've probably destroyed any fingerprints the sheriff might have been able to use."

"Not necessarily. There's still the cassette inside. Maybe whoever left it got careless."

"But—but why didn't Andy act concerned?"

"Probably because he knew the sound was fake," Smith said. "If it had been real, he'd have behaved differently."

Julie Ann's jaw gaped. She snapped it shut. "You're right. I never thought of that. He'd be able to tell, even if I couldn't. He does the same thing with animal noises on television."

"You weren't really going to open the door, were you?" To Smith's chagrin she nodded, looking contrite and more than a little embarrassed.

"I'm afraid I was. If you hadn't called when you did and stopped me, I'd have been out on the porch."

"With whoever left the tape as bait," Smith added, unable to mask his displeasure and concern. "You know better, yet you were going to come outside? I don't believe it."

To her credit, she didn't look any happier about her near escape than he did.

"Humph," she said, making a face. "I don't believe I was going to do it either, but I was." She began to smile slightly. "I guess we're even now."

"Even?"

"Yes. I saved you after you were shot. And you just saved me from who-knows-what."

"We don't know that for sure," he argued, more for her sake than because he truly believed it, although he did lower the pistol for safety's sake.

She glanced at the tape player, then back at Smith's face. Stepping closer, she reached to gently, briefly caress the day-old whisker stubble on his cheek. "*I* know it. And you do, too, so don't try to deny it. You got here just in time to keep me from making a very serious error in judgment."

"Maybe nothing would have happened," he replied with a heavy sigh.

"Nevertheless, thank you," Julie Ann said, backing away. "I'd ask you in for a cup of coffee but…"

"I know. No chaperone. I understand." Turning, he'd started to descend the porch stairs when he was seized by an unexpected wave of dizziness. Leaning against the handrail, he stuck the Colt in his belt so he'd have a free hand and paused for a moment to regain his equilibrium.

Julie Ann was beside him in an instant. "What's wrong?"

"Nothing. I'm fine."

"Fine, my eye. Are you dizzy?"

He shrugged. "Maybe a little. It passes."

"You're *not* going to drive home."

"I can't stay here. You said so yourself."

She winced. "I did, didn't I? Well, what are we going to do? I'm certainly not going back into the house and leaving a sick man sitting out in my driveway. What kind of Christian would I be if I did that?"

"The sinless kind?"

"Right. That'll be the day."

"You could bring me a blanket and I could just wrap up and lean the car seat back and…" Smith could tell by the expression on her face that she was not going to go for that idea.

"I'll get my purse and drive you home."

He scowled. "And then what? Come back here to a house that's been sitting empty? That's not very safe."

"It's no different than coming home after work or jury duty. Besides, Andy'll be here. He'll watch for prowlers. And I'll take Grandpa's gun with me so that when I come back I'll be armed, too."

"Oh, that's real comforting."

"It is to me."

Smith rolled his eyes and felt another surge of dizziness. He wasn't in a position to argue, nor was he sure she was wrong. If he passed out behind the wheel, he'd be an even bigger fool than she was. And, in his opinion, that was *huge*.

As Julie Ann left him and hurried back inside to fetch her purse and the old revolver, Smith watched her go. Appreciation filled his heart and soul. She was a remarkable woman, wasn't she? She displayed a maturity about life that most twenty-five-year-olds lacked. He'd hate to have to go against her in a battle of wills.

That thought annoyed him. They were already engaged in such a battle and she was winning, although only because he was hurt. At least that was his excuse. And he planned to stick to it until he came up with a more plausible one.

Looking around at the deserted yard, he was struck by all the places where an assailant could hide in ambush. He could not let her come home alone, nor was there any way he could convince her that she should remain in town tonight. For once, he wished she were not quite so morally upright.

"No, I don't," he countered, upset with himself for even thinking such a thing. Julie Ann was a good woman, through and through. The kind of person he might someday choose to be his wife. That notion hit him between the eyes like a sucker punch. Wife? Julie Ann? Just because they had come to rely upon each other more lately, that didn't mean she was the woman he needed beside him for the rest of his life. Did it?

The wind had started to blow, heralding another spring storm. Smith cradled his injured arm and shivered. He'd think about the future later, when he was certain he even had one to share with her.

The way it looked at present, they'd both be fortunate to see the sun rise on next week, let alone on the years to come.

Julie Ann had scooped up the tape recorder when she'd passed it on the porch and brought it along. It now lay on the console between Smith's seat and hers, while her purse and the old, holstered pistol occupied the rear one.

She surreptitiously watched him as she drove. As far as she could tell in the dim illumination from the streetlights closer to town, his color was improving.

Other than that, Smith hadn't given her any reason to believe he was feeling better. He hadn't spoken except to give one-word answers to her queries and she hadn't even been able to get him to argue. Therefore, she assumed he was still feeling rotten.

"Where do you want me to let you off, by the front door or around back so you don't have to climb so many steps?"

"The front is fine. I'm not an invalid."

"I never said you were. I do think, however, that you had better not drive again until the doctor says you can."

"Opinion noted."

"But not taken, I assume," she said, giving him a lop-sided, knowing smile. "Why am I not surprised?"

"Probably because you're even more stubborn than I am," Smith told her.

"I am not." The declaration had no more than passed her lips when she realized how contradictory it sounded. "Well, okay, maybe we're equal."

"I consider that a compliment," he said.

"Really?"

"Yes. Really." He opened the door of the SUV and paused with one foot on the ground. "What now? Are you going to give that tape player to Harlan and tell him the latest?"

"Yes. I'll stop by his place on my way home and turn it over to him. I don't care if someone was just playing a sick joke, I still want him to have it as evidence." And besides, now that I think about it, maybe my TV remote was stolen so I wouldn't be able to accidentally mask the crying noise with the television, which means this was no simple prank. Whoever planned it was deadly serious. And they were inside my house, at least long enough to set that up, she thought.

"Smart lady," Smith said. "Is the sheriff's office open all night?"

"No. It doesn't have to be. I know where Harlan lives."

"Okay," Smith said. "Even if he and Boyd have already gone to get your car, I want you to keep using this one, at least for tonight. Drive it home and let me know when you're safely locked in again. Promise?"

"I promise. But don't wait up. I intend to stay at Harlan's long enough to make sure he takes me seriously."

She shivered from her nape to her toes when Smith stared at her and said, "I think, in view of this bullet hole in my arm, he'll take anything you say a lot more seriously from now on."

"You should never have come out tonight," she said tenderly, touching his good hand. "It was dumb."

"I agree. But you left me no choice."

"Let's just say that whoever was fooling around out at my place is responsible, okay?"

She was relieved when Smith said, "Okay."

Julie Ann watched him slowly climb the stairs, cross the porch, and let himself into his house. She hated to leave him like that but what else could she do? If she lingered instead of returning in the light of day, there was no way she'd escape the gossip that was sure to follow. It wasn't as though she planned to do anything wrong, it was merely a case of not giving the *impression* of wrongdoing.

Until recently she hadn't understood the importance of that scriptural admonition. Now, however, as she considered Smith's shaky medical condition and her intense desire to look after him, it became all too clear.

What she needed, she reasoned, was someone to come along and check on him with her; someone like Louella. She brightened at the thought. That was the answer! She'd ask Louella to enlist the aid of some of the more mature ladies from their women's Sunday school class in looking after Smith, at least temporarily. Then no one would think there was anything improper going on.

Right now, she had a date with the sheriff. Harlan

might not appreciate being rousted out of bed in the middle of the night but that was too bad. If he'd caught the people responsible for the damage to her window and her tires, not to mention whoever had shot Smith, she wouldn't have had to knock on his door at two in the morning.

"This better be good." Evans had been awakened by the ringing of the bedside telephone and was not in a pleasant mood.

"It's me, boss. Melvin."

"I hope you have something good to report. Did you get rid of another juror?"

"Naw. I almost had the one that I missed when she was crossing the street with the old lady. The plan was working great till her boyfriend showed up."

"What boyfriend?"

"The guy I winged out at French Town. Those two have been thick as thieves since this whole thing with Lester started. She was about to come out of the house when he drove up and interfered."

"So, forget her. Choose a different juror. Aren't there others you can get to just as easily?"

"Not really. I picked her because she lives so far from town. And because I'm getting sick and tired of her getting away. That place out in the country is perfect. I can sneak around all I want without being spotted."

"You're sure nobody saw you?"

"Not a soul," Melvin replied. "Which is why I didn't try to do her and the boyfriend at the same time. Close-in like that, they might of seen my face. If one of them escaped, they could ID me and then I'd have to stop going to the trial."

"That makes sense. You didn't leave any clues behind?" The silence on the other end of the line was momentary but telling.

"Well, not exactly," Melvin finally answered. "I mean, nobody can trace it to me. It was just an old tape player. When the real estate guy drove up, I had to leave it on the porch where I'd hid it. How was I to know they'd both leave and take it with them?"

"Get it back," Evans ordered. "I don't care what you have to do, just get it."

"Yes, sir." Melvin snorted. "It's not like I dropped a rifle or anything. I mean, there's no way to trace the stupid tape machine any more than there was to figure out whose shotgun killed Denny. If we hadn't tricked Lester into showing up at the storage yard and handling that gun after I shot the kid, they wouldn't even have *him* to blame."

"Stop making excuses. This is not open to discussion, understand?" Evans muttered a curse. "Do you even know where the tape machine is?"

"Matter of fact, I'm following it right now. As soon as the girl gets out of that big car, I'll grab it."

"Be careful. Like you said, if she IDs you…"

"She won't," the hired killer said with a coarse laugh. "I've got a score to settle with her. She won't be in any shape to identify her own grandma by the time I get through."

ELEVEN

Julie Ann was deep in thought as she drove toward the sheriff's house. She could picture herself banging on his door and being greeted by his predictably irate, portly personage. Too bad she hadn't thought to alert him before she'd left home. And, to complete a lovely evening, it was beginning to rain again. Terrific.

Large drops began to plop against the car windows and leave streaks in the dust. She slowed the SUV as she neared her next turn. A vehicle that had been rapidly approaching behind her also slowed, blinding her with its headlights.

She turned on the windshield wipers, then reached up and changed the rearview mirror to the night driving position. Still, the SUV's large side mirrors reflected blinding beams that glistened off the increasing rain, causing her to brake again for safety's sake.

The other vehicle matched her reduced speed perfectly. Julie Ann's heart began to race, her pulse pounding in her temples. Why didn't they pass? There was plenty of room, no cars were coming from the opposite direction and the rain wasn't heavy enough to hamper visibility that much. Yet.

Hoping to encourage the other vehicle to go on by, she eased toward the shoulder of the road. By peering into her side mirrors, she was finally able to make out the size and shape of a light-colored pickup truck rather than a car, which explained why the headlights were set so high off the ground.

At least it isn't a black Humvee, she thought, relieved. "Come on. Pass me. I've given you lots of room."

And still it remained behind her. Close behind. Frighteningly behind. Tellingly behind. She shivered. This was beginning to look less like a normal traffic situation by the second.

Now what? She didn't dare pull over any farther, nor was she going to try to outrun an unknown nemesis again, especially not on slick pavement. Yes, she knew every street and alley in Serenity but maybe this pursuer did, too. It was only by the grace of God that she and Smith had escaped the last time. Fleeing at high speed through town was not a logical option. Neither was stopping to get the gun from the backseat and making herself a better target. Besides, there was still a chance that her imagination was simply playing tricks on her because she was so overwrought.

She accelerated evenly, watching her mirrors. The truck also sped up. For a few blocks, it kept pace. Then, it suddenly surged ahead and banged into her rear bumper.

The jolt took her by surprise. Nevertheless, she held tightly to the wheel and maintained a steady course. She thought briefly about possible damage to Smith's SUV, thanking the Lord that his vehicle was substantial enough to take that kind of punishment without giving ground.

The truck fell back, then came at her again, even faster than before.

Julie Ann was ready. She quickly hit the brakes, taking her adversary by surprise. The pickup slammed into the sturdy rear bumper. Hard. Glass shattered. Metal crunched.

"Gotcha!" she shouted, still in full control.

The instant she felt the force from the collision ebb she took her foot off the brake and floored the accelerator. The powerful SUV's tires spun for an instant, then caught. She shot forward.

Her hands gripped the wheel. She strained against the shoulder strap of the seat belt, leaning into the curves. As far as she could tell, she'd left the other vehicle behind. Nevertheless, she didn't intend to stop until she got to the sheriff's home.

She was going so fast by the time she turned onto Possum Trot Road she almost overshot Harlan's place. Brakes squealing, she made a hard right into his driveway and immediately killed her lights.

Had she been seen? Was she still being followed? It was hard to tell for sure if she'd given that truck the slip. There were no headlights visible on the otherwise dark road. Then again, she had definitely heard glass breaking the second time he'd hit her, so maybe his lights were permanently knocked out.

Trembling, Julie Ann made certain that all the car doors were locked and sat there for a moment, listening to the rain, watching for movement along the otherwise deserted street and struggling to control her emotions.

If her adversary had not actually collided with her, she might have laughed off the encounter and convinced herself it had not been a true assault.

Since the person had hit her twice, however, she knew there was no mistake. It had been an attack, all right. And if she had been driving her own little car when it had happened, she very easily could have been pushed off the road and into a ditch. Or worse. Especially since it was now pouring rain. Thank heavens she had taken Smith's advice—and his car.

Her hands were trembling when she leaned on the horn to announce her arrival. It wasn't a polite toot, it was a panicky, repetitive blare. And she didn't stop sounding it until the lights inside the sheriff's house came on.

Harlan finally appeared at the front door. Judging by the size and shape of the shadow at his side, he was armed.

His wife, Edith, stood behind him, belting a fluffy, white terry-cloth robe that matched the one her husband was wearing.

Julie Ann summoned her courage, bolted from the SUV and raced toward them, waving her arms and shouting, "It's me. Don't shoot!"

Edith Allgood put an arm around Julie Ann's shoulders, ushered her into the living room and sat beside her on the chintz-covered sofa. "Now, now, dear. You're perfectly safe. Tell us what's brought you out on such a nasty night."

She pushed her damp hair back with a shaky hand. "I—I feel like a baby for being so scared."

"Nonsense," Harlan said gruffly. "You're entitled. You've been through plenty, of late. What brings you here? And how did you get Smith's car?"

"It's a long story," Julie Ann said, suddenly remembering the things she'd left in the SUV. "I have more proof of a prowler to show you. It's outside. Come with me?"

"I'll fetch whatever you need," the sheriff said. "Just let me go pull on a pair of pants so the neighbors don't call the law on me, okay?"

She knew he was trying to lighten her mood by joking so she forced a smile. "Okay. I suppose it's safe enough for a few minutes."

As soon as he returned, dressed, Julie Ann stood to accompany him. He waved her off. "You stay put. I'll take care of whatever's in the car so you don't get any wetter than you already are. Just tell me what to look for."

"I'm not afraid of a little water."

"Then we'll all go," Edith said, picking up an umbrella. "If the neighbors don't like the looks of my robe, that's just too bad. I'm as covered up as I ever get." She stood firm in spite of Harlan's chastening glance. "Well, I am. And you know it."

Julie Ann stayed under the shelter of the umbrella with Edith and let the sheriff take the lead. The older woman was still mothering her. Rather than being off-putting, that extra attention felt good. Julie Ann hadn't had a very close adult relationship with her own mother and father, and until she'd joined Serenity Chapel and become a part of that church family, she hadn't felt truly at home anywhere. It was that same feeling of belonging, of being cared for, that she was experiencing through Edith's ministrations.

"I don't think I remembered to lock the driver's door when I got out in such a hurry," Julie Ann called to Harlan as he reached to open it. "Look on the console between the seats. We found that tape player on my front porch. You won't believe what's on the tape."

The sheriff leaned in, then straightened. "Where did you say it was?"

"On the console." She quickened her pace to join him, oblivious to the downpour. "Maybe it fell off. I was driving pretty fast."

He unlocked the other front door and started to search that area while Julie Ann checked the backseat.

Her eyes widened. The tape machine wasn't the only thing missing. Her purse was right where she'd laid it, but Grandpa Willis's holster and pistol were gone!

Smith took a dose of his prescription antibiotic and pain medication before he plopped into his reclining chair, leaned it back and put his feet up. As his granny used to say when she was overly tired, he felt like he'd been run through the ringer of an old-fashioned washing machine.

"Probably fighting a fever," he muttered. "That's all I need. If I get sick I'll have to drop off the jury, and with Estelle in the hospital they'll use up their last alternate."

He looked at his watch, hoping to see that morning

was near but finding the opposite. It would be at least three more hours before he could safely phone Logan Malloy without waking him and ask him to have Becky or one of the other church women look in on Julie Ann. Smith knew she wouldn't like that kind of interference, no matter how sensible it was, but it was worth getting scolded in order to help insure her safety.

In addition, he reminded himself, he didn't dare sleep until she'd called as she'd promised to let him know she was home.

He sighed and closed his eyes, totally spent. The drone of the rain on the roof provided soothing background noise. Brightly colored lights danced behind his lids. It had been past time for his medication when he'd finally taken it and he was paying for the error. Just a few more minutes of rest, he told himself. Just a little relaxation. The throbbing in his arm was starting to ebb, thanks to his prescription, and he was beginning to feel a bit better.

When he opened his eyes again, it was dawn.

He bolted upright. Something was terribly wrong, but *what?* He couldn't put his finger on it. He'd just rested his eyes for a few minutes and then...

Julie Ann. That was it. She hadn't called. She couldn't have. There was a phone sitting on an end table next to the sofa. He'd have heard that ringing even if he'd been sound asleep. There were no new messages on his answering machine, either.

"I never should have left her, gossip or no gossip," Smith reprimanded himself. "I should have stayed outside in the car and stood guard."

"And do what?" he argued. "Fight for her with one arm in a sling and your head splitting with the worst headache of your life. You couldn't even pull the slide to cock your .45 without two good hands."

Boy, was that right. Barely able to concentrate through the haze of pain, he stood. It was time for another dose of his medicine but finding out about Julie Ann came first.

He redialed her home number and let it ring fifteen times before he hung up and called 9-1-1.

By the time Boyd answered at the sheriff's office, Smith was perspiring heavily.

"Julie Ann Jones may be in trouble," Smith blurted. "She was supposed to call me last night and didn't."

Boyd's chuckle in response raised the hairs on the back of Smith's neck and made him grip the receiver tighter.

It wasn't until the deputy said, "She's fine, Smith. Spent the night at Harlan and Edith's," that he was able to relax.

"Are you sure?"

"Yep. Positive. The sheriff took her out to French Town first thing this morning to pick up her car. Since he isn't back yet, I guess she's not, either. Wouldn't worry, though. He'll prob'ly follow her back to town, what with the roads out that way bein' all muddy and everything."

"Okay. Thanks." Weak with relief, Smith sank back onto the couch. *Safe.* She was safe. Praise God.

Maybe it was time he started going to church again, he mused, repeatedly thanking the Almighty in his heart. He was well aware that he'd done more than his share of praying of late, especially in regard to a certain young woman whose life had become so intertwined with his. Perhaps he'd go to Julie Ann's church. He might even see her there.

That image was so vivid it surprised him. He'd done many things to impress women in his younger days, including attending their home churches, but this was different. For some unfathomable reason he really wanted to go to Serenity Chapel—*with* Julie Ann. And since he was afoot and also on medication, it wouldn't be out of line to ask her for a ride.

He basked in a feeling of triumph even before putting his plan into action. He already had the perfect reason to phone her. Once they were talking, he'd casually mention church and ask her to pick him up on Sunday when she brought his car back.

It was a flawless plan—until he looked outside and saw his SUV already parked in the driveway.

After Julie Ann and the sheriff had dropped off the SUV on the way to French Town to pick up her car, Harlan had followed her to her house so she could tend to Andy and Bubbles before returning to Serenity for the day.

Although she had not been able to hand the sheriff the proof she had had in the SUV, she could tell he'd believed her whole story this time, even the abstract reasoning behind her missing TV remote.

What upset her, almost as much as knowing that a stranger had been in her house, was losing Grandpa's gun. Whoever had stolen it had left her purse behind, indicating that the crime was not a simple robbery. However, since the tape player and the pistol had been taken, she had to assume that her nemesis was now in possession of both. It was less than comforting to know that Harlan agreed with her conclusion.

She had intended to call Smith the night before, as promised, but in all the confusion it had slipped her mind. By the time she did remember, several hours had passed and she had assumed he'd be asleep again. Since he desperately needed his rest, she had decided to see him the following morning instead of phoning.

As she pulled into his driveway and got out of her car, he flung open the front door and stepped out onto the porch.

Overjoyed to see him, she grinned, waved and called, "Hi. You're looking much better this morning."

"No thanks to you," he said flatly. "Why didn't you let me know you'd changed your plans?"

"Things didn't go the way I'd expected," she answered, hurriedly joining him. "I'm sorry if you were worried. You won't believe what happened after I dropped you off."

"Boyd said you spent the night with Edith and Harlan. I'd have rested easier if I'd known."

"There's a lot more to it than that. It was unbelievable."

She'd stepped nearer to Smith as she'd spoken and wasn't surprised when he slipped his good arm around her to draw her closer. Although she had not actually planned for him to do so, she had secretly hoped he might.

She laid her cheek on his chest and felt the vibration

of his heartbeats. They were rapid. So were hers. In fact, they seemed to be keeping perfect time with each other, as if their minds and hearts were somehow in sync. To her delight and surprise, he placed a kiss on her temple and she felt his warm breath ruffle her hair.

"So, what made you decide to stay with the Allgoods instead of going home? Was it the stormy weather?" he finally asked. "And what did Harlan have to say about that tape player we found?"

Julie Ann gazed up at Smith so she could interpret his expression as she explained. "It's complicated. There's a little damage to the rear bumper of your SUV. I'll be glad to pay for the repairs."

"Damage? Why?"

The color drained from his face when she answered, "Because somebody followed me and smashed into it." Pausing to let that much sink in, she added, "And whoever it was got away with the evidence *and* my grandpa's gun."

Thunderstruck, Smith held her at arm's length. "When?"

"Right under the sheriff's nose. I'd parked your car in his driveway and gone inside for a few minutes. When we all went back for the tape player, it was gone and so was my pistol."

"Are you sure it happened there?"

"Positive. I never left the vehicle until then. I suppose things could have turned out worse. My purse wasn't taken," Julie Ann said. "It was on the backseat in plain sight and wasn't touched."

"So, this wasn't a normal robbery."

"That was Harlan's conclusion. And mine."

It was all Smith could do to subdue his temper in the face of her blasé attitude. Didn't she know how much danger she'd been in? Didn't she care? It was all his fault. He should have stayed with her just as he'd kept telling himself.

"Was the bumper damaged during the robbery?"

"No." She made a face. "Actually, I was passing through town when I started to suspect that a truck was following me. At first, I thought he was just afraid to pass. After he rammed into the rear of your SUV for the second time and smashed his own headlights, I got the idea it was no accident."

"Did you get the license number?"

"No. It was behind me and it was too dark. I could see that it was light-colored and pretty old. Come to think of it, it was like the one that hit Estelle."

Smith had to struggle to choke down the scolding he wanted to give her for getting herself into more trouble. Logic told him it wasn't Julie Ann's fault that so much had happened to her—and to him. He couldn't prove it, of course, yet there was little doubt in his mind that Lester's trial had to be the key.

The question then became, what could anyone do about it? If a mistrial was declared due to the lack of a full jury, would the threat be gone or might it intensify? There was no way to predict. Nor was there any guarantee that a quick guilty verdict would end the persecution they were experiencing, especially if he was wrong about the underlying reason for the attacks against them.

If he could have done anything, said anything, wished anything, it would have been to free Julie Ann of the constant threat that was hanging over her. Over all of them.

TWELVE

Julie Ann was reluctant to leave Smith's embrace, particularly since he wanted to discuss the accident and that subject made her even *more* nervous than usual. Nevertheless, she chose not to follow when he stepped away and began to pace the porch.

"Suppose we try to retrace your path from last night and look for evidence?" Smith said. "If the guy who was chasing you really did smash up his truck there should be glass or something on the road. It can't all have been washed away by the rain. At least I hope not."

"The sheriff said he was going to look in the area where it happened but he didn't seem to think he'd find anything useful." She glanced at her watch. "We'll have to get a move on if we're going to do that. My first appointment is at nine and it's already after seven."

"Wait a minute. You're going to work? After all that's happened? Do you think that's wise?"

"Only if I want to keep paying my bills and eating on a regular basis," she said. "Somebody has to keep Bubbles and Andy in kibble."

"I understand. I just thought…" He hesitated. "I could loan you some money to tide you over, if you're short."

"I'm always short," Julie Ann replied with a half smile. "At least that's what Ben used to tell me when he was teasing me about my height."

"You know what I meant."

Her smile faded. "Yes. I know exactly what you meant. You're beginning to sound just like my mother. She's been telling me for years that I need to find a nice, rich man to take care of me, the same way she did, instead of working and trying to succeed on my own." Julie Ann huffed. "For the record, I have no intention of giving up my freedom or putting myself in a position where I have to ask any man's permission to buy a new dress or get my hair done."

Smith's brows arched and he held up his good hand, palm out. "Whoa. I was offering a loan, not proposing marriage." He gave her a lopsided smile and shook his head. "Guess I touched a sore spot, huh?"

"You could say that."

She knew her cheeks were flaming. She averted her gaze, mortified by her outburst.

"It's all right," Smith said. "I'll know better next time."

"Will there be a next time?"

"You mean because you told me off just now? Sure. I have broad shoulders. I can take it."

"Good. Because I have been known to dish it out pretty thick. I'm working on becoming a perfect Christian but I'm not there yet."

"You're close enough," he replied. "Which reminds

me, I was wondering if you'd mind picking me up for church."

"You don't have to go that far. I'm not mad at you."

"I'm not asking because you got testy. I want to go. I'd thought about it long before you showed up this morning."

"You had?"

"Yes. I'm not even upset because you didn't phone me last night." He shrugged. "Well, not much, anyway. If you insist on going to work today, I'm staying right with you. No arguments. Okay?"

"*Very* okay." She started to back away. "First, let's retrace my steps and see what we can turn up."

"You're not afraid to be seen poking around?"

Julie Ann straightened her spine and shook her head. "Not if you're with me."

Evans was furious. "So, you got the tape player back. Don't expect a bonus for cleaning up your own messes."

Melvin pressed his lips together and held his temper. "I told you I'd take care of it and I did."

"What about the truck you banged up again last night? Did you ditch it for keeps this time?"

"Yeah. It's out on my uncle's hunting land. Nobody'll stumble onto it there. Even deer hunters steer clear of his place. Too many hidden pits and limestone caves."

"All right. As long as you're sure there's no way to trace anything you've done, I want you to cool it for a few days. Take the rest of the weekend off. Let the local yokels calm down and get secure again."

"What about Monday?"

"If the trial resumes then, you'll have to play it by ear. Like I told Lester's lawyer, we want to drag things out for the time being, not end it and start over. Listen to the testimony, and if it looks like the jury is going to be asked to decide about the old man, then thin the jury pool again."

"How?"

Evans gave a coarse, sinister laugh. "How, is up to you. That's what I pay you for. You're doing pretty good so far."

Smith let Julie Ann drive the SUV once again as they started cruising the still-damp streets to look for clues. She handled the larger vehicle well and the less he had to move his arm, the better he felt.

"Did you ever tell Harlan about those two suspicious-looking old men we noticed in the courtroom?" she asked.

"Yes. He knows who they are and he said he was sure they wouldn't actually try to hurt any of us."

"Humph. They didn't look that innocent to me."

"Assuming they're responsible for all the problems, no," Smith said. "But according to the sheriff, all our friends from court would admit to was letting air out of your tires. They were cooling their heels in jail in Mountain Home during the time when I was shot. They'd driven over there to buy beer and apparently sampled too much of it before they got all the way home."

She cast a brief glance at him. "Hmm. Interesting. Maybe their main interest in Lester was the stuff he brewed in his still."

"That's what Harlan seems to think."

"Do you agree?"

Shrugging, Smith shook his head. "I don't know. It makes sense only if you assume there's more than one bunch of crazies stirring up trouble. The question is, who and why? Maybe if the prosecutor offers Lester a plea deal, he'll talk."

"Not unless he really killed Denny," Julie Ann countered. "Remember, he's innocent until proven guilty."

"He was standing next to Denny's body, holding the shotgun, when Boyd drove up and caught him. How much more proof do you need? He has no alibi."

"We don't know that he pulled the trigger. There wasn't any gunpowder residue on his clothing."

"Not that they found," Smith reminded her. "Our local sheriff is a great guy but he's not equal to a city crime lab. If he needs a real technician to gather evidence, he has to send all the way to Little Rock for one."

"Edith says he took a class a couple of years ago."

"And uses what he learned how often? Once a year? Less? I'd be surprised if he's had enough practice to be considered proficient in crime scene investigation techniques."

Julie Ann sighed. "I suppose you're right." She slowed the SUV and pulled to the far right-hand side of the two-lane, country road. "I was near here when that truck hit me the first time. Then we went about another half mile. That's when he smashed his headlights."

"Okay. Take it slow." Smith was squinting against the bright sunlight, shading his eyes with his good hand, and peering at the muddy, rock-strewn roadbed.

"There!" He pointed. "Something's sparkling like glass."

"You're right. Did you bring a plastic bag?"

He reached into the loop of the sling and pulled out a sandwich-size baggie. "Right here. How are we going to pick up the pieces without touching them?"

"Come on. I'll show you." She parked, then quickly climbed out, heading straight for the shards of glass. Taking the baggie, she slipped her hand in and deftly turned it inside out to use like a mitten. "See? No fingerprints."

"Clever. Did you learn that from Harlan?"

Julie Ann chuckled. "Nope. Mystery novels. I knew my interest in whodunits would pay off someday."

Standing aside, Smith kept his eye on the road to make sure no other vehicles were approaching that might endanger Julie Ann. A glint in the weeds along the edge caught his eye. At first he thought it was just a reflection off the water droplets. Then, as he got closer, he could tell it was a piece of metal.

"Over here," he called, pointing. "Is that chrome?"

"Looks like it. Hey, maybe the sheriff will hire us as crime scene investigators."

"I sure hope not," Smith said cynically. "I've had just about as much crime scene as I can take. Especially when you and I are the stars of the show."

"You're right about that." Approaching the curved piece of chrome she managed to lift it, untouched, by using the upper portion of the same baggie. "This looks like the trim that goes around a truck's headlight."

"I'm not sure what good it will do," Smith said with a shrug. Unexpectedly nervous, he kept looking around, scanning the woods and nearby houses, even though there was no one else in sight. "Come on. Let's get out of here and turn that stuff over to Harlan."

"What's your hurry? I still have a little time before I have to be at work. Maybe we'll find more clues if we poke around in the weeds."

"No." Smith was adamant. He took her by the arm and urged her back to the SUV in spite of her protests.

"Wait a minute. What's the hurry?"

"I feel like we're being watched and I don't want to hang around out here any longer than necessary," he explained, practically shoving her into the car with his good arm.

He was relieved to see that she was finally taking his concerns seriously because she slid behind the wheel as he circled to the passenger side and got in.

"Okay, okay. Just let me stick this stuff in the back and…"

"Put it in the console the way you did the tape player. It'll ride fine there." He pointed to the ignition key. "Let's go."

Smith was aware that he'd frightened her. Although he couldn't explain his instinctive reactions to their surroundings, he *knew* they'd been in imminent danger. He'd had the same kinds of uneasy feelings out at French Town, just before they'd been shot at, and had mistakenly attributed them to his emotional response to Julie Ann's unexpected arrival. He wouldn't make the same error again. If being a Marine had taught him anything, it was to trust his instincts for survival. Sometimes, that was all the warning a man had.

Smith glanced at her as she drove. Her hands were gripping the wheel so tightly her knuckles were white, and her eyes were wide in spite of the bright, morning sun. He wasn't any more relaxed than she was. The hairs on the back of his neck wouldn't stop prickling.

Had they really been in danger? Only God knew, Smith told himself. If the Almighty had spurred him to act, to get them out of there, fine. If he was simply overreacting to the stimulus of the accident the night before, no harm had been done. Either way, they were almost to the sheriff's office and would soon turn over the evidence they'd found.

Smith wished it were that easy to be rid of the obligation to sit in judgment of Lester Taney. As long as either he or Julie Ann was still involved, he wouldn't have a moment's peace. None of the jurors would.

He cast a sidelong glance at the young woman seated next to him. He was beginning to feel as if their lives were so inevitably connected they would always remain so. Was that logical? She had sure felt right when he'd held her in his arms that morning. More than right—she'd felt wonderful.

Smith shook his head and pressed his lips into a thin line as he considered their budding relationship. As long as there was so much shared jeopardy to color and confuse their feelings, there was no way to tell if she'd hugged him because she was just scared or because she cared for him. When things settled down and got back to normal, there would be plenty of time for him to think about Julie Ann and building a possible future with her.

Until then, looming threats of danger would continue to be what drew them closer and that wasn't a reliable gauge of how either of them truly felt.

As he pondered the past weeks, Smith shivered. Denny was dead, Estelle was still in the hospital and he had been shot. It was only by the grace of God that Julie Ann had escaped another bullet, the trap on her own porch and the attack while driving. If anything happened to her he didn't know what he'd do.

One thing was certain. Right now, she was the most important person in his life and growing more dear by the minute.

She must have sensed his attention because she briefly glanced at him, raised her eyebrows when their eyes met, and asked, "What?"

Smith shook his head. "Nothing."

"You look awfully solemn for a man with nothing on his mind. You didn't see any new threats, did you?"

"No. Nothing like that." Fighting to appear unconcerned he managed a lopsided smile. "I didn't know I looked glum. I thought I was just enjoying the scenery."

"Serenity is a pretty little town, isn't it?"

"Yeah," Smith said, reaching for her hand and clasping it gently so there would be no confusion when he added. "The town is nice to look at, too."

They'd dropped off the evidence they'd collected and gone directly to Serenity Salon from the sheriff's station. To Julie Ann's chagrin, the front door of her shop was locked and the Closed sign still in place.

While Smith hovered behind her, she dug in her

purse for the keys and murmured, "I don't understand it. Sherilyn should be here already."

Turning the key in the lock, she opened the door and found the shop deserted. As she flipped the sign on the door she called out a hello. No one answered.

"Maybe she was unavoidably delayed," Smith offered.

"I hope it was unavoidable. I'd hate to think I've lost my only employee. Sherilyn is kind of different but she's always been reliable."

He huffed. "Different? That's putting in mildly. I never could figure out why you hired her."

"To begin with, I was doing a favor for Brother Logan. It turned out to be a good decision," Julie Ann said. "Sherilyn was one of his rescue projects and she needed a job, so I put her to work as soon as she finished beauty school."

"She'd been in trouble?" Smith asked, eyebrows raised.

"Nothing serious. Just the same kind of petty things Denny and his buddies used to be involved in." She bit her lip, thinking about Sherilyn's confession regarding the young man's visits while she was working.

"Denny ended up dead," Smith said, tensing.

"And Sherilyn had been seeing him."

"Seeing? As in, dating?"

"I'm afraid so. She told me she was in love with him."

"At her age she was probably in love with love."

Before she could squelch the urge to equate her own teenage mistakes with those of her employee, Julie Ann cast a quick, telling glance at Smith. Judging by the contrite expression that suddenly came over him, he had just made the same connection.

"I wasn't referring to you," he insisted.

"Hey, I was just as crazy back then as Sherilyn is now. Thankfully I have my head on straight these days."

"Glad to hear it."

Julie Ann wasn't sure she was nearly as glad as Smith had sounded. There were some aspects of her teen years that she missed terribly, such as the adoring feelings that being near him had engendered. Feelings that were bubbling nearer and nearer to the surface since he'd held her hand so recently.

Her teeth clenched. Those same tender emotions were still dangerous, only now she was better able to subdue them and keep from embarrassing herself—and him. Every time she thought of all the ways she'd thrown herself at the poor man years ago, not to mention the love letters she'd penned, she was mortified.

Working her way through the shop, she checked her answering machine before heading for the storage room to make sure she had adequate supplies in stock. When she opened that door and spotted her employee, curled into a fetal position on the floor, she almost screamed.

Her gasp of surprise was enough to draw Smith to her side. "What is it?"

Relieved to see that the girl was alive, Julie Ann crouched beside her. "Sherilyn? Are you okay?"

The teen was almost catatonic. Smith helped Julie Ann lead her out of the closet and guide her to one of the chairs beneath a dryer.

It was clear to Julie Ann that Sherilyn had been weeping because her eyes were puffy and her nose was red, just like the last time she'd become hysterical.

"What is it?" Julie Ann clasped her clammy hands and stroked them the way a mother comforts a frightened child. "Tell us. Let us help you."

Sherilyn finally lifted her gaze and focused on her boss. "You can't help me. Nobody can."

"Try me."

When she got no positive response she looked toward the front window. "You're not still scared because somebody was shooting at me, are you?"

Sherilyn swallowed a sob. Her fingers clasped Julie Ann's so hard it hurt. "That's just it," she stammered, wild-eyed. "They weren't shooting at you, they were shooting at me!"

THIRTEEN

Julie Ann's glance met Smith's. She could tell he was as confused as she was. She patted Sherilyn's hand. "You must have been imagining things."

"No. I'm sure. They told me."

"*Who* told you?" Julie Ann asked.

"D-Denny's friends. They thought I said something about Lester that made him shoot Denny. They said they wanted to scare me so I wouldn't tell on them, too. But I couldn't. I don't know anything. Denny never said a word."

"About what? Tell us. We won't get you into more trouble. I promise."

At that, the girl gave a cynical laugh that became another sob. "You can't get me into any more trouble than I'm already in. I swear, I don't have a clue what Denny was doing. All he said was that he was working for a really important guy and that we were gonna be rich."

Looking at Smith, Julie Ann arched a brow. "That doesn't sound much like Lester Taney."

"It sure doesn't. Go on, Sherilyn. What else can you remember? Anything at all," Smith prompted.

"I don't know." She paused to blow her nose and blot her tears. "He did mention trips down to the flats, so maybe this rich guy wasn't from around here."

"A flatlander? Now we're getting somewhere," Smith said. "What else?"

"Um, I don't know. There was never anything like a whole story. It was just bits and pieces of little things. Funny things. Like all the times he was gone and wouldn't tell me where he went. And once, when he was putting gas in his car down at the quick stop, he just started laughing for no reason, like he was crazy or high or something. When I asked him what was so funny, he asked me if I wanted a drink. I thought he meant a soda so I said yes, and he laughed harder."

"Did he go get you a soda?"

Sherilyn shook her head. "No. I figured that was just because he was broke, from buying the gas, you know, so I offered to pay. He acted like I was making a big joke."

"Okay," Julie Ann said. "If you think of anything else, anything at all, call me. I'll be right here all day. In the meantime, I want you to go home and get some rest."

The girl's eyes widened. "I can't go home. They know where I live."

"Then go to Brother Logan's. Becky will take care of you and tell you what to do. She did before."

Wiping her eyes repeatedly, Sherilyn shook her head and hunkered down in the chair. "I can't go outside. They'll shoot me."

"If they'd wanted to do that, they'd have done it before, instead of warning you," Smith said wisely. "I can call the sheriff and get you an escort if you want."

"No! I don't dare be seen with the law. Don't you get it? I'll look like I'm ratting them out. *Again.*"

"Okay. Calm down. We'll drive you to Brother Logan's. It'll only take a couple of minutes."

"You go," Julie Ann said. "I have a million things to do here." Noting his hesitancy she added, "You said it would only take a few minutes. So, go do your good deed for the day. I'll be fine till you get back."

The expression on Smith's face was unreadable. He scowled at her. "Like you were fine last night?"

"That was in the dark, not broad daylight. Besides, my first customer will be here any second." It was only a slight exaggeration, one Julie Ann permitted herself to make for the sake of her own sanity. If she didn't get a break from Smith's presence soon she was afraid her self-control might snap.

Besides, she reasoned, what could happen to her midmorning in a busy shop?

The answer to that question came in the form of a list of possible catastrophes that zinged through her mind with lightning speed. She turned away to keep Smith from discerning her unreasonable apprehension. As long as she stayed busy and didn't give in to her overactive imagination, she'd be okay.

But what about the *real* dangers? she asked herself. Those were still out there. Even if the shots through the shop window had been meant to frighten Sherilyn, that didn't explain the rifleman who had drawn a bead on Smith. Or the Humvee chase. Or the driver of the tan pickup who had run down Estelle and then tried to wreck Smith's SUV while Julie Ann was behind the wheel.

Whoever had done that was more of a threat than a gang of young men with overly superior attitudes and some petty crimes to hide. Whoever had killed Denny was still out there. Still a very real menace.

Those disturbing thoughts continued to whirl around in her befuddled brain while Smith took her hand and tugged her toward the door.

In view of the things she'd just considered and the disturbing conclusions she'd reached, she figured it might not be such a bad idea to go with him to Brother Logan's after all. Her poor business was already going down the tubes. What was one more late appointment among so many that she'd had to cancel in order to fulfill her civic duty? For once, she was going to listen to her heart. Calling, "Wait! I'm coming, too," she grabbed her purse and followed.

The rest of Saturday passed in a blur. Sunday morning came early, long before Julie Ann felt rested. The times she had slept she'd dreamed of Smith, or of danger, or both. She was far from ready to face picking him up for church. If she hadn't already promised to do so, she would have been sorely tempted to pull the covers over her head and go back to sleep.

She smiled and yawned as he joined her in the car. "Morning."

"Good morning. Am I keeping you up?"

"Yes."

"Sorry about that. How about letting me take you out to dinner after the service? That is, unless you're worried about starting more gossip."

Julie Ann shook her head. "We're going to sit in church together. I don't think there will be any way to avoid rumors after this morning."

"You could stop and let me out so I could walk in and pretend I don't know you," he said, grinning over at her.

"There's no need. We aren't doing a thing wrong."

"We never were," he replied. "Our only real problem seems to be that we've made enemies and we don't have a clue who they are."

She stifled a shiver and pressed her lips into a thin line. "I can't imagine it's anyone we know. I mean, folks in Serenity just don't do things like that."

"Lester made moonshine. Brother Logan told me he thinks the whole affair revolves around that, although he hasn't been able to tie any of the loose ends together. Neither have his contacts in law enforcement. They have assured us that our sheriff is totally honest."

"Poor Harlan. No wonder he's so confused," Julie Ann said. "He's not privy to the kind of advanced information system Logan can tap into."

"True. Still, you and I should be able to sense if someone is scheming against us."

"Not if they're strangers." She huffed. "And speaking of odd things, look at that up ahead of us. You don't see many limos around here."

"No kidding. Can you get a little closer to it? I want to read the license plate."

"Why? Are you looking for wealthy clients?"

"Always." He leaned forward, squinted and read the plate aloud. "NRG 1. I wonder where it's from."

"Probably down in the flatlands between here and Jonesboro," Julie Ann said. "I understand there's a lot of alternative energy manufacturing over that way."

Smith asked, "Wonder what he's doing way over here?"

"Slumming," she gibed, then sobered to add, "Sorry. That wasn't very Christian of me. Guess I'm not perfect yet, huh?"

"You'll do," Smith told her. "I hope the roof of the church doesn't cave in when I walk through the door. I'm not exactly a regular."

"Were you ever?"

"When my grandparents made me go with them, I guess you could say I was. After Grandma died, Grandpa didn't go out very often. He only lived a year or so longer than she did."

"I'm sorry." Touched, she decided to reveal brief details of her own home life. "I've always wondered about that kind of devoted couple. My mom and dad don't seem to care about each other much. I think that's even sadder than what happened to your grandparents."

"Not all marriages are as bad as they may look from the outside," Smith said with evident empathy. "My parents weren't nearly as close as my grandparents, yet I know they loved each other. After my dad died and Mom remarried, I think it was because she missed him so much, not because she didn't care."

Julie Ann refrained from commenting. It was comforting to assume that others had found the kind of happiness she could only dream of. Such things might be attainable but she had no idea how she could be certain she wasn't making a terrible mistake or choosing a mate for the wrong reasons.

In her opinion, that was exactly what her own mother had done. If Julie Ann hadn't learned anything else while growing up in a household with a dominant father and weak-willed, subservient mother, she had learned to be plenty cautious about making permanent choices in life.

Those unsettling thoughts brought her to consider the man seated beside her in the car. Smith Burnett wasn't as bossy as her father had been but he did have a stubborn streak. Of course, she was not a clone of her mother, either. On the contrary, she was…*contrary.*

That play on words made her smile.

Smith echoed her grin. "What's so funny?"

"I am," Julie Ann admitted easily. "Tell me, do you think I'm obstinate?"

His resulting laugh echoed inside the small car and caused her to arch her eyebrows.

"Can I take that as a *yes?*" she asked wryly.

"Not on your life," Smith said as he fought to control his amusement. "I know better than to say or do anything that goes against your independent nature."

"Ah. It was a yes. Good. I'm glad we understand each other."

"Do we? Do you know me well enough to know what I'm thinking, Ms. Jones?"

She gifted him with a smile while keeping her eyes on the church driveway when she said, "I doubt it. No more than you know what I'm thinking about you."

"Is that good or bad?"

Julie Ann wheeled into a parking place and stopped before she looked him in the eyes and answered. "I'm not sure. Ask me after the trial is over." Assuming you and I both make it through this whole ordeal alive.

The thought made her shudder. Being totally honest with herself, she realized she was more concerned about Smith's well-being than she was for her own safety. And, sadly, there was no way she could help protect him, particularly since he was hampered by his injured arm and she no longer had Grandpa's gun. There must be something she could do. But what?

She paused and voiced her decision. "Okay. We'll have dinner together after church if you want, but then I want to go back out to French Town and look for more clues."

"That's crazy." He was frowning and shaking his head. "It may be safe enough to drive along a well-traveled road and pick up a few scraps of glass, but it's stupid to go traipsing around in deserted ruins, miles from town, especially after what happened to us the last time we were out there."

"Fine." She quickly got out of the car. As soon as he joined her she added, "If you won't go with me, I'll go alone."

"No, you won't. I won't let you take the risk of being out there alone. I'm coming along for the ride."

Julie Ann huffed, but secretly was pleased. "Fine."

"Come on," Smith said, taking her hand. "Let's go surprise Brother Logan and ask him how Sherilyn is doing, then find a pew to share and give the congregation even more to talk about."

* * *

In spite of her desire to do things her way, Julie Ann had to admit that driving Smith's SUV out to French Town, as he had suggested, was the smartest choice.

"I don't know about eating our chicken dinners in here," she said as they bounced down the dirt road toward their destination. "We'll get your car messy."

"Not a problem. We'll open the back and have a tailgate party."

"I wish I had my gun," she said, slowing as they approached where Smith had parked the last time they'd been there.

"I'd have had mine with me if I hadn't been going to church. If you're worried, we can go back to town and get it." He raised his good arm in a calming gesture when she stared at him. "Just a suggestion, not an order."

"Ha! I'd be more likely to take you seriously if you didn't tease me so much. I'm really not that hard to get along with, you know."

"Well…" His lazy drawl was accompanied by a smile.

"If you didn't have a sore arm I'd smack you the way I used to do my brother," Julie Ann said.

"How's Ben doing? He's always been bad about writing and I haven't had a letter from him in ages."

"Neither have I. We had kind of a falling-out before he went into the service."

"Really? What about?"

"Ben and I had a disagreement about the damaging influence of Denny Hanford and some of his other friends. If Ben hadn't left town when he did, he might have kept hanging around with the same people and gotten into trouble the way Denny did."

"Well, at least you know Ben has straightened up now. Besides, it didn't seem to hurt you any."

"I've explained all that. Denny and I just shared some of the same friends. There was nothing personal between us." One eyebrow arched and she looked over at Smith. "You didn't believe me?"

"Not entirely, no. I sensed that there was something you were holding back and I wasn't sure what it was."

"Well, now you know. Denny was always a wild kid and Ben tended to go along with his crazy ideas. It was only a matter of time before Denny's poor choices caught up with him—and his friends. That's another thing that's been bothering me. Nobody's acted interested in the bad company Denny was keeping. What about the guys who threatened Sherilyn?"

"Logan said he was going to talk to them privately before informing the sheriff," Smith explained. "He didn't think they were as dangerous as they pretended to be."

"But why was Lester involved?"

"I don't know. Do you think he was framed?" Smith asked.

"Sure looks like it to me."

"That's a pretty simplistic conclusion." He smiled wryly. "Not that I'm arguing with you. Besides, if the judge knew we were discussing the trial we'd probably be in big trouble."

Julie Ann couldn't help returning his smile. "You'd never dare argue with me, would you? At least not out loud."

"Well, you did say I was smart."

"Right. Although I have to disagree with you about jury rules. We're not looking for clues to Lester's crime, we're just trying to figure out who shot at us." Easing to a stop in the shade of an oak, she turned off the engine and purposely changed the subject. "Hungry?"

"Starving. I'm surprised you couldn't hear my stomach growling during the sermon."

"I thought that was my own I was hearing. Before we eat, let's take a quick look around the place where I think the shots came from so I can relax and enjoy my food."

"Okay, but if I keel over from hunger, it'll be your fault."

"Very funny. The last time we were out here you hit the ground for another reason and I don't even like thinking about it."

"Sure you do," he countered. "You want me to remember that you rescued me so I'll feel indebted."

"Do you?"

"Oh, yeah. I may even nominate you for a citizen's award of valor. Get you a big, shiny medal and a framed certificate and…"

"I hope you're joking."

"Yes. But you do deserve praise. You handled yourself very well in a tough situation."

"Thanks." She'd been leading the way to the wall where she'd been standing when she was fired at. Now, she pointed. "The first bullet hit up there, among the vines. You can't see the spot because of the leaves but I saw a puff of dust and felt little pieces of rock falling."

"Where was the shooter?"

"Over that way, I think," she said, swinging her arm in an arc. "Maybe we'll find some shell casings if we go look."

She could tell that Smith was not enthusiastic because he started lagging behind before they were halfway to the higher ground where she was convinced the assailant had lain in ambush.

"Come on. It'll only take a few minutes," she insisted.

He lightly touched her forearm. "Wait. Listen. Do you hear another car?"

"Could be. It's a Sunday afternoon. There are probably lots of folks out on four-wheelers and in Jeeps and such, seeing the country and soaking up the sunshine."

Still, Smith held her back and his demeanor was so serious, she chose to let him have his way. The more she listened, the more she had to agree with his assessment. It sounded as if whoever was out there with them was drawing closer.

When he tugged on her arm and urged her to take cover, she complied by ducking behind a low wall with him. "I feel silly hiding," she said, making a face. "Why are you so nervous?"

"Maybe I'm influenced by the bullet hole in my arm. Humor me for a few minutes, at least till we see who's driving around out there."

Just then, a squat, black, all-terrain vehicle, exactly like the one they had eluded at Saddle, crested the ridge where Julie Ann had been headed.

She gasped, ducked lower and peeked between the leaves of the vines covering the rough stone. Her breath was raspy, her voice quavered. "Look! He's getting out."

"I see that. Keep your head down." Smith grimaced. "Sorry. I mean, *please* keep your head down."

"Sounds like a good plan to me no matter who thought of it," she whispered. "He's looking for something."

"I agree. I wish we'd brought binoculars."

She shivered. "We don't need them. I can tell what he's picking up. It's brass shell casings."

"I think you're right."

"I know I am." She was gritting her teeth. "If only we'd come out here right away instead of stopping to buy dinner, we could have picked up that evidence before he got to it."

"No way, lady. Whoever that is might have caught us snooping around. He's the last person we'd want to inform that we're on his trail. Remember what happened the last time?"

"I know. I just wish I could see his face better. That baseball cap makes too much of a shadow."

"Maybe we can read his license plate when he turns around to leave."

"Maybe. It would be easier if Arkansas required plates on both the front and rear, the way some states do."

She fidgeted impatiently, waited until the other man climbed back into his vehicle, then left her hiding place and ran toward the ridge.

She knew Smith would have yelled at her if he'd dared make any noise, but at that moment she didn't care. All she needed was one quick look at that plate.

Just a glimpse. Even if she didn't manage to see or remember all the numbers and letters, she had to try.

The black vehicle was moving slowly, of necessity, as it maneuvered off-road among the boulders. Julie Ann ducked behind a tree, then peeked out. The rear plate was only visible for a split second. That was enough.

She sagged back against the rough bark and waited for Smith. As soon as he joined her she blurted, "You won't believe what I saw. That license plate. It said, NRG 3. There has to be a connection to the limo we noticed in town this morning."

"Are you sure that was what it said?" Smith stepped closer and slipped his good arm around her shoulders.

Breathless, she gladly leaned into his embrace. Between her dash to the ridge and the shock of finding out that there was undoubtedly more than one element involved in their predicament, she was in need of his comfort, his support.

"Positive," she said. "This is not some small-town vendetta against jurors who are supposed to be judging a good old boy like Lester Taney—or some dumb kids shooting out a window to scare a teenage girl. It's much bigger. And whatever's going on, we're stuck smack-dab in the middle of it."

FOURTEEN

Harlan was clearly unhappy to hear about Julie Ann and Smith's additional sleuthing. He did, however, issue Smith the promised permit for a concealed weapon and made a vow to look into their suspicions.

As far as Smith was concerned, that was sufficient. To his dismay, Julie Ann had other ideas. He shook his head vigorously when she voiced her opinion as they sat in the Serenity Community Park and finished their cold chicken dinners.

"No," he said. "That's not sensible. I don't care if you did look over the sheriff's shoulder when he found more details about the NRG corporation on his computer, we have no business going anywhere near their ethanol facilities. Especially not now that we've made a possible connection."

"That's exactly why we should take a closer look," she argued, wiping her fingers on a napkin. "There has to be a reason why those flatlanders are spending so much time driving around up here. Do you think that man from the Humvee was picking up spent cartridges just because he collects brass? Give me a break. Besides, we owe it to Lester and to Denny to figure out what's going on."

"What we owe them is a fair trial as part of an impartial jury. We're already over the line. Once Harlan tells the judge what we've been doing, we'll both probably be booted off the jury for misconduct. And it would serve us right."

"Aren't you the least bit curious?"

"Sure, I am. I just don't intend to stick my nose into something that's none of my concern. Let the sheriff handle it. It's his job."

"I know that. But Edith says Harlan can't get directly involved if an investigation takes him out of Fulton County, so whatever he does will have to be handled through the Craighead County sheriff." She began to smile as she gathered up their trash and dumped it in a nearby refuse can. "You and I, however, can go anywhere we want."

"*Want,* is the operative word, Ms. Jones." He stood and joined her as they started back toward his SUV. "No matter what we may wish would happen, we have no right to behave like the investigators on some TV show. They get to come back each week for a whole season no matter how dumb they act. We're living a real-life drama here. We could get hurt." Or worse, he added, hoping that his argument was sufficiently sensible to sway her opinion.

"That's overstating the problem," Julie Ann countered. "All I want is to drive out to the NRG plant and look it over. They probably even offer public tours to promote their alternative fuel. It'll be a cinch to get inside."

Smith rolled his eyes. The woman was impossible.

Once she got her teeth into something she held on like a dog with a bone. No wonder her brother had been so insistent that she needed someone to look after her. "You're not going to give this up, are you?"

"Nope." She checked her watch. "It's early yet. If we leave now we'll have plenty of time to travel there and back before dark."

"Assuming everything goes smoothly."

She slid behind the wheel. "What can go wrong?"

"Lots of things. More than I care to think about," Smith replied. "But if you're not going to change your mind, I'm going with you."

"Okay. But just this once."

As Smith sat back and watched Highway 63 play out in front of them, he began to worry, then turned to silent prayer. *Father, I haven't been very good about asking for Your advice recently but I'm asking now. Help me. Help us. I don't know what to do, or not do, and I could really use some guidance.*

Expecting divine peace, he was disappointed. The closer they drew to Craighead County in the Mississippi delta where the NRG plant lay, the more his gut tied in knots. And the more he wished he'd insisted they delay long enough to stop by his house and pick up one of his personal firearms.

By the time Julie Ann took the well-marked turnoff that led to the actual ethanol manufacturing complex, Smith's nerves were so frayed he could barely keep from grabbing the wheel and insisting they turn back.

The only thing that kept him from doing so was his sure conviction that such a move would only spur her to make an even more rash decision—one that could put her—put them—in a worse situation than they were already facing. If there were such a thing.

Although Julie Ann was chagrined to find the expansive parking lot empty, she pulled into a spot and stopped the car nonetheless. "Rats. I had hoped they'd be offering weekend tours."

"Not likely on a Sunday. Not in the Bible Belt," Smith countered.

"You're right." Hesitating, she glanced over at him. "What now?"

"Hey, don't look at me. This was your idea, remember?"

"I know. I just thought…"

"No, you didn't think. You reacted," he said. "And I was fool enough to come with you."

"I never forced you to do anything."

"Yes, you did."

Getting more frustrated by the moment, she made a face at him. "Oh, yeah? How?"

"By insisting you were coming out here alone. What did you think I'd do, give you my blessing and the keys to my car? Let you do this all by yourself, after everything that's happened?"

"You could have."

"No, I couldn't," Smith said flatly. "And you know it."

She was taken aback. "You really feel that strongly about it?"

"No," he said, staring into her eyes as he explained. "I feel that strongly about *you*."

She could sense something much deeper than simple concern, see love in his eyes. And this time it wasn't all her imagination. He did care. Deeply. And she must have known it, at least on a subconscious level, because she had used that love to coerce him into coming with her.

"I'm—I'm sorry," Julie Ann said softly. "I didn't realize…" She stopped herself. "No. That's not true. I did know you cared for me as much as I cared for you. And I took advantage. I apologize."

"Good." Smith was peering at the seemingly deserted plant. "Then let's turn around and get out of here."

"Well, we are already here and…"

"No way, lady. We're leaving."

"I just thought I'd have a quick look around. You know, see if I could spot either of those vehicles we saw in Serenity today." She'd been watching her companion's handsome face as she'd spoken and wasn't surprised that his jaw was set and his expression of fondness faded.

"Don't look at me like that," she said, shaking her head. "Nobody's here. We can just walk up to the fence and have a quick look."

"There are bound to be guards."

"Then we'll pretend we're tourists. I'm sure it happens all the time. No one will know who we really are." As she finished speaking, she opened the door and slid out. Without waiting to see if Smith was following, she started toward the perimeter fence.

There were Keep Out notices hanging next to the padlocked entrance gate. More elaborate descriptive signs explained what the plant did and how it was helping the environment by making clean, alternative fuel.

Julie Ann shaded her eyes and peered through the chain-link fencing. She sensed Smith's closeness when he joined her. "I don't see any activity," she said aside. "I guess this is hopeless."

"Good. Now let's go."

"And you say I'm stubborn. You have a one-track mind, mister."

"Only with regard to self-preservation," he replied. "My arm reminds me every time I move it."

"Okay." She shrugged. "I'll give up and do it your way. I don't see how we can tell anything more without going inside, anyway. I just hate to quit."

"Don't think of it as quitting," Smith countered. "Think of it as sensibly staying out of trouble."

"That sounds like something I used to tell Ben."

"It was good advice." He gently took her hand as they turned and started back to the SUV. "And speaking of Ben, when all this is over, you and I need to have a serious talk."

"About Ben?"

"No, about me."

Something personal? She shivered in spite of the warm, late afternoon sun. The touch of Smith's hand was light and unassuming, yet it affected her all the way from the top of her head to her toes. This was no longer the silly crush of a lovesick teen. She was ready to admit she cared for him as an adult and she was certain he could tell.

Like it or not, it seemed that the more she fought her

feelings, the stronger they grew. What was wrong with her?

There was just something special about believing Smith cared and was willing to put himself on the line for her. Suddenly, she felt his grip tighten.

He held her back with force as he said, "Look."

Julie Ann's breath caught. She stopped so abruptly she almost stumbled, and would have if Smith hadn't steadied her. An all-too-familiar black Humvee had entered the lot and was barreling straight for them. Even if they'd been close enough to Smith's SUV to make a run for it, it probably would have been useless to try to outmuscle such a formidable foe. Or outshoot them, for that matter.

Smith stepped up and tried to shove her behind him but she stood her ground.

"I'm not going to hide or act guilty," she told him firmly. "We haven't done one thing wrong. It's not trespassing to be here."

When he said "No, but that doesn't mean we're not in serious trouble," she realized how dreadfully right he was.

Smith stood stock-still as the passenger from the black Humvee got out and approached. He had expected to be questioned about their reasons for being there and was going over plausible excuses in his mind. Unfortunately, he wasn't given an opportunity to explain anything.

He felt Julie Ann's grip on his hand tighten as she whispered, "He's got a gun."

"I see that," Smith replied, quietly speaking aside to her. "Don't move."

"I don't think I could if I had to."

Their nemesis gestured with the heavy black automatic in his hand. "Turn around."

"We were just..." Smith began before being cut off.

"Shut up. We know what you've been up to. We followed you here. Now get moving."

"Where are you taking us?" Smith asked, hesitating.

The taller, heavier man laughed hoarsely. "Inside. You wanted to see what was going on and you're about to get your wish. March."

As if to emphasize the command, the driver of the Humvee gunned the engine.

Smith slipped his arm around Julie Ann's shoulders as he shepherded her toward the entrance gate, as ordered. "If there weren't two of them, I'd tell you to make a run for it," he whispered. "But the guy behind the wheel is likely to run you down if you try."

"I know. I was thinking the same thing." She leaned even closer. "If you get a chance to make a break for it, yourself, don't hesitate. The keys are still in the ignition."

"I'd never leave you."

He saw her manage a wan smile and he tightened his hold on her shoulders as she said, "I know."

The pungent odors in the interior of the plant reminded Julie Ann of a cross between a bakery and a distillery. She blinked, her eyes smarting from the fumes. "Whew. You can sure tell what they make here, can't you."

Smith nodded. "Yes. I imagine it smells a lot like Lester's moonshine still."

Scowling and wiping her eyes she stared at him. "What did you just say?"

"Moonshine?" He paused, evidently thinking, then shook his head. "No. That's not plausible. The Feds would be all over this place like bees on honey if they tried to peddle any of this stuff for drinking."

"But, is it possible?"

"Chemically, I suppose so. There's not much basic difference between corn liquor and the ethanol manufactured for fuel. Toxins are added to prevent human consumption, but that doesn't mean it would be poisonous when it's freshly distilled."

They were directed down a dark hallway and into an office. A silk-suited executive was seated behind an enormous desk bearing a nameplate that read George Evans, Plant Manager. He didn't rise when they were ushered into his presence. In fact, he looked more than merely perturbed. He looked angry.

"Melvin, you're a first-class idiot. What do you think you're doing?" he asked. His piercing, gray gaze was focused on the man holding the gun.

"I caught them snooping around outside."

"And that was enough to make you bring them to me? Now they know what I look like, you fool."

"Yeah, but boss, they were poking around out at French Town again today."

"How do you know that?"

"Um, 'cause I was there, too. I remembered what you said about not leaving any clues and I figured I'd better pick up all my shell casings. That's when I spotted their car. They didn't see me, though."

"They're here. Obviously they saw *something*." He pushed back his leather chair and stood slowly. "I had hoped to avoid any more bloodshed. Now, thanks to you, it seems inevitable."

Reaching for an intercom, he ordered another man into the room, then waited beside the thug who was still pointing the gun at Julie Ann and Smith. As soon as a younger guard entered, Evans gave him hushed orders and then left with Melvin.

Julie Ann was confused and so frightened she could barely function, yet she couldn't help thinking that the newly arrived guard looked vaguely familiar.

As she studied his round, freckled face, she grew more and more positive that she had seen him before. Where? Serenity? Had he been another of Ben's cronies? And if so, what was his name? If only she could remember.

Judging by the way the blond young man was peering at her, she assumed he must be having similar thoughts. Did she dare ask? Maybe if she pictured him with longer hair and the slighter build of a teenager it would jog her memory.

She made cautious eye contact with the guard, hoping and praying he wasn't as nefarious as his cohorts or the man they all worked for. He seemed fairly nice, in a menacing sort of way. She took a chance. "Don't I know you?"

Remaining stoic, he shook his head.

"Are you sure? I'm Ben Jones's sister, Julie Ann."

She could tell from the arch of his eyebrows that he *did* recognize the names. Her heart sped. She held her breath, then released it with a noisy whoosh and glanced at Smith to see if he'd been paying attention.

His barely perceptible nod told her he hadn't missed a thing. She smiled at him in spite of their dire situation. He was so dear, so special to her. Although she realized that his life was on the line, too, she was secretly glad that he was with her. She didn't want anything bad to happen to him, of course, she just couldn't help cherishing his influence, his strength, his mere presence. It felt as if the Lord had sent him for the express purpose of guiding her through this dark valley, this incredible danger.

The guard's cell phone rang. He answered.

Julie Ann watched his countenance change. For the first time since he had entered the office, he looked unsure of himself. His gaze darted first to Smith, then settled on her as he spoke into his phone. "But… Yes, sir. I understand."

Sensing bad news, she eased closer to Smith, not wanting any distance between them when they learned of their fate. She was too young to die. She had barely lived. And what about those children she'd never have?

When the guard used his gun to gesture toward the door, Julie Ann leaned against Smith and whispered a prayer for deliverance.

She knew he had heard her and was agreeing when he pressed a kiss to her temple and softly said, "Amen."

FIFTEEN

As they were herded down the otherwise deserted hallway at gunpoint, Smith tried to keep himself positioned between the guard and Julie Ann, not that he could see any way to prevent their mutual demise in the long run. He was a good enough judge of character to know that the young man had just been given orders which troubled him greatly. That was one point in their favor, although clearly not enough to guarantee survival. The only other possible way out was if Julie Ann had been right when she'd suggested a past association.

That didn't ensure that the guard could be swayed, of course, it merely provided a potential avenue of escape. When she began to mutter first names, he knew she was thinking along those same lines.

"Sam? Tim? Jim?" Julie Ann murmured. "No. More unusual. I think it was…Cam! That's it." She turned to the younger man and her voice rose. "You're Cam Phelps. I remember you. You used to have long hair and you were a lot skinnier when you hung around with my brother, but I know it's you."

Smith had been casting sidelong glances over his

shoulder, watching for a reaction. When he saw the color drain from the guard's face he stopped walking and spun on his heel. "What are you supposed to do with us, Cam?"

"I—I..."

"Never mind. You don't have to answer. I can see it in your eyes. You don't want anything to do with murder, do you?"

The guard shook his head.

"Then *help* us," Julie Ann blurted.

"I can't. They'll kill me, too."

Smith had a ready answer. "Not if we knock you out and get away." He cast around for a suitable weapon, saw nothing and made a fist with his good hand. "If you cooperate and don't duck, I can hit you hard enough to be convincing."

Glancing at one corner of the ceiling near the far end of the hallway, Cam lowered his voice. "You'll have to make it look real good. There's a surveillance camera up there. They'll have the whole thing on tape."

"Okay. Suppose Julie Ann knocks your gun out of your hand and then I punch you? Will you let her do that and not accidentally shoot?"

Cam's nod was barely perceptible. "I don't have my finger on the trigger anyway."

"Good." Smith glanced at Julie Ann. "Ready?"

She tensed. "Yes. Are you?"

"As ready as I'll ever be."

She jumped into action so quickly that Smith was almost caught by surprise. Nevertheless, he stepped up and swung in time to catch Cam off balance and connect solidly with the point of his jaw.

The slighter man collapsed like a marionette whose strings had been snipped by a giant pair of invisible shears.

Smith rolled him over, grabbed a small pouch from his belt and tossed it to Julie Ann before helping himself to the guard's GLOCK automatic and tucking it into his belt. "There are spare ammo clips in that case so don't lose it," he shouted. "Let's go!"

Wheeling, they took off running. Now that they were aware of the cameras, Smith knew their time to make good an escape would be severely limited, especially if someone was monitoring their every move.

The hallway seemed endless. Their footsteps echoed as they pounded down the corridor. Smith had a pretty good sense of direction and had kept track of the number of turns they'd made when entering, yet he knew it was easy to get confused in the midst of wild flight.

Julie Ann started to go the wrong way at an intersection. He grabbed her wrist. "No! This way."

"It's this way," she insisted, resisting.

"No, it isn't." Smith set his jaw, tightened his grip and yanked her after him with a terse "I don't have time to argue with you."

He could tell she was far from convinced but this was one instance when he was so right he'd have staked his life on the decision. As a matter of fact, that was exactly what he was doing.

To his relief, she began to keep pace beside him. "Here," he finally shouted, letting go of her so he could hit the door with his good shoulder.

Julie Ann straight-armed the door as well and they found themselves back in the parking lot.

Gasping for breath they raced toward his SUV. Smith was ecstatic to note that the black Humvee that had followed them from Serenity was nowhere in sight.

"Can you drive?" Julie Ann shouted.

He faltered and almost grabbed her arm again. "Are you hurt?"

"No," she yelled. "I'm just too shaky."

"All right."

Smith yanked open the driver's door, praying that the keys were still in the ignition and that their enemies had been so sure of themselves that they hadn't seen any need to disable the vehicle.

He slid behind the wheel and turned the key. The engine caught. His heart soared. They might actually get away!

Clenching the steering wheel with both fists he shouted to Julie Ann. "Hang on! Here we go."

She had barely made it into the passenger's seat and pulled her safety belt over her right shoulder when Smith gunned the engine and dropped the SUV into gear. She knew she'd made the right decision by asking him to drive because her fingers weren't obeying her mind enough to even engage the seat belt latch. If she couldn't manage that, she was certainly in no condition to handle evasive driving.

Bracing herself for the turn back onto the highway, she glanced over at Smith and saw him using both hands as if his arm hadn't been injured. "Are you doing okay?"

"Fine. Get that belt on."

"I'm trying."

As they took the first corner, tires squealing, she

pressed her feet hard against the floorboard to help hold her body in place. Her heart was fluttering and her breathing ragged. She had never been more frightened in her entire life. It was just now sinking in how close they had been to dying. Both of them. And if they didn't get out of this mess in one piece, it was going to be her fault.

Smith straightened the wheel and floored the gas pedal. The acceleration pressed her back into the seat like the g-force of a jet plane on takeoff but at least it provided enough slack to allow her to finally latch the seat belt.

"What are we going to do?" she asked, needing to talk, to hear his voice, more than anything else.

"We're doing it," Smith shot back.

She saw his firm jaw, his hands tightly grasping the wheel. "Isn't your arm hurting?"

"No."

"Liar."

"This is hardly the time or place to argue," Smith countered. "We'll have plenty of time to talk when this is all over."

Julie Ann was positive she could read a deeper meaning behind his simple statement so she answered in kind. "I want to have time. Time for *us*."

He didn't take his eyes off the road. "We will. I'll get you out of this. I have to. In case you don't already know it, I *love* you."

"I was hoping you'd say that."

"You were?"

"Yes."

"You love me, too?"

"Yes, and if I wasn't so stubborn, I'd have already admitted it." She would have grinned if she hadn't been worried that those might be their last moments on earth. "I really blew it eight years ago, didn't I?"

"That was then. This is now," Smith said. "You were too young to know what you were doing. And I wasn't about to take advantage of that weakness."

"You were protecting me?"

"Yes. I was."

Realizing the truth of that thought, she sobered and decided to speak from the heart. "I guess I never stopped loving you no matter how much you used to ignore me, you obstinate, impossible man."

"That was sweet," Smith gibed. "You never give up, do you?"

"Nope. I can't help myself. What you see is what you get."

"Good."

He cast a momentary glance her way and she could see telltale moisture in his eyes before he added "Because I just spotted a black Humvee behind us and he's coming up fast."

Julie Ann twisted, straining against the seat belt.

Smith was right. The men from the ethanol plant were hot on their trail. "What're we going to do?"

"Keep running. This highway is full of little towns with speed traps. If one of them doesn't catch us, maybe they'll at least nab the bad guys."

"God willing," Julie Ann said. "I never thought I'd end up praying to be stopped by a traffic cop!"

* * *

Smith had checked every side road, every truck stop and every café parking lot as they'd passed through Portia, Imboden, Ravenden and all the rest of the small towns where he'd expected police intervention. There hadn't been a patrolman in sight in any of the usual places.

He had, however, managed to safely pass several other vehicles also traveling the narrow, curving road and thereby lengthen the distance between them and their pursuers.

Julie Ann had assumed a sideways position and kept an eye on the road behind, giving him steady bulletins regarding their status in relation to their enemies.

"I can only catch glimpses of them when we go around the corners," she said. "But I'm sure they're still back there."

"No doubt. How are you doing?"

She huffed. "Not great. I think I'm kind of carsick."

"Turn around and watch the road ahead. We don't know how far we'll get before we're forced to stop and you need to be in shape to run."

"Run? On foot?"

"Yes. We'll split up. I'll try to lead them away."

"Uh-uh. No way, mister. I'm not leaving you and that's that."

"Be sensible. They can't follow us both."

"Sure they can. If there are two of them back there, like before, it won't do us a bit of good to split up this time, either. Like you said back at the NRG plant, they can each chase one of us."

He concentrated on quickly maneuvering around a

left-turning pickup truck, then continued their conversation. "As much as I hate to admit it, you're right. Which means we have no other choice but to stay on this road and try to make it back into familiar territory."

"Maybe then Harlan will believe us."

"That's it!" Smith shouted. "Call Harlan. Tell him to meet us and be ready for a showdown."

"I don't have his number. If I call 9-1-1 from here I'll get the wrong department."

"They can relay the call. My cell phone's in the pocket of my jacket."

She had to undo her safety belt in order to lean over the front seat and reach the jacket. "Got it." Opening the little phone she stared.

"What's the matter?"

"No service. Can you believe it? Just when we need it, there's no cell service."

"There soon will be," he told her. "I always have a strong signal closer to Hardy. Just be patient."

"I hate to tell you this, Mr. Burnett. Patience is *not* one of my virtues."

Smith couldn't help chuckling in spite of their dire situation. "Could have fooled me," he said, hoping that his efforts at lightening the mood would help distract her, at least superficially. "And here I thought I'd found the perfect woman."

"You have," she replied, her focus still on the screen of the small cell phone. "God just has a few rough edges to polish off yet. I'm real close to flawless."

It was the hint of amusement in her tone that told him she was back to being her normal self—reliable, resilient, intelligent and ready for anything life threw at her. He just hoped she'd be able to forgive him when he finally confessed that his initial interest in her was due to a battlefield promise he'd made to her brother.

His fists tightened on the wheel. This was no time to bring up anything like that. Their ultimate survival depended upon their ability to continue to work together, just as it had when they'd turned the tables on their armed guard at the NRG plant. The last thing he wanted to do was say something that might alienate her.

"Three bars!" Julie Ann yelled.

"Wait for four," Smith replied. "Then you'll be sure they understand exactly what's going on."

He thought, studying her expression, that she might dispute his sensible conclusion.

Then, when she lowered her hands to her lap, sighed deeply, and kept staring at the phone, he realized that for the first time in as long as he could remember, she was not only going to listen to his advice, she was going to take it.

Wow, he thought, awed. She really does love me.

"What're we supposed to do when we catch 'em?" the driver of the Humvee asked. "We can't just shoot 'em in public and expect to get away with it."

"I've still got that old gun I lifted from the girl. It'll make a perfect, untraceable murder weapon," Melvin replied.

"If I can catch up to them."

"You will. Then we'll force 'em in here with us so we can take 'em out in the country somewhere and get rid of 'em once and for all."

"I can't believe Cam let those two get away."

"Neither can I. We may have to settle with him, too, once we get back to the plant. For now, I'll keep watching the side roads so we'll be sure they don't turn off."

"Looks to me like they're makin' a straight run for Serenity."

Melvin nodded. "Even if they get there it won't matter. There's only two regular lawmen in that whole county and they can't be everywhere at once."

"How do you know they won't be out lookin' for us?"

Laughing, he spat out his open window. "Because, the boss is going to send 'em off on a wild-goose chase, clear over to the Baxter County line. The sheriff won't get in our way no matter how long it takes us to catch up to those two nosey jurors."

SIXTEEN

"This is Julie Ann Jones," she shouted as soon as the phone was answered.

"You have reached the Craighead County sheriff. State your emergency," the dispatcher droned as if he were so bored he could hardly keep from yawning.

"We're being chased. By guys with guns!"

"Please, calm down and speak clearly. What's your present location?"

"Um—we're on the highway, almost to Hardy."

"That's Sharp County, ma'am. Please hold. I'll transfer your call."

"No! Wait! I want…"

Smith scowled at her. "What's the matter?"

"He didn't listen. He's transferring me. Can you believe it?"

"That's okay. You wanted to talk to Harlan anyway."

She rolled her eyes and made a face. "Yes, I did, only that's not who he's transferring me to."

"Just take it easy," Smith said. "Don't panic. We won't be in Fulton County for another twenty minutes or so."

He was right, of course. She pressed her lips together

and tried to stay calm despite growing aggravation. By the time the call was answered by the second dispatcher, she had better self-control.

"We're almost to the Fulton County line," Julie Ann said after briefly explaining their situation. "Sheriff Allgood is familiar with this case and with both of us. Just tell him Julie Ann Jones and Smith Burnett need his help and he'll understand. We're on Highway 62/412, about to turn toward Serenity from Ash Flat."

"I'm sorry, ma'am. Your signal is breaking up. Would you repeat that last part?"

She tried, received no confirmation, and looked to Smith. "I think they got it but I'm not positive. We lost the signal."

"Keep trying. Maybe you can reach Harlan directly as we get closer."

Julie Ann fought back unshed tears. If they couldn't find help before they reached Serenity, it wouldn't do any good to be home. Even considering the gun Smith had taken from Cam back at the NRG plant, they were still outnumbered.

They could die just as easily in Serenity as anywhere else.

Cam Phelps regained consciousness where he'd fallen after Smith had punched him. His head was spinning and his jaw felt as though it was broken but that was nothing compared to the mess he realized he was in.

Now what? Who could he turn to? There had been no one in Serenity who had believed in him when he was growing up; no one except Logan Malloy. Brother

Logan was a regular guy, real down-to-earth for a preacher. A man Cam now felt was his only hope.

He couldn't find the GLOCK that he always carried while on duty and was therefore defenseless, so he spent a few minutes wandering through the plant looking for the other weekend guards before he concluded that he'd been left alone. Good. That meant he could safely make a call to his former pastor and get his advice before leaving the premises for keeps.

His basic instincts told him to make a run for it and never look back. His conscience insisted that more was required of him.

Stepping out into the twilight of the parking lot he flipped open his cell and dialed the still-familiar number of Serenity Chapel. It had been several years since he'd called Brother Logan, yet the number was as clear in his memory as any other. He didn't stop to wonder why he recalled something that obscure. He simply knew that he was doing the right thing. Finally.

Julie Ann was so on edge that she couldn't help breathing hard and trembling in spite of the fact that all she was doing was sitting there, riding beside Smith.

"I'll try again," she said, punching the buttons of the little phone with one manicured nail. "Harlan has to answer. He just has to."

"Maybe you should use up some of your excess energy by praying," Smith said.

"That's all I've been doing since we left poor Cam," she countered. "I hope he's going to be all right."

"When this is over, we can tell the authorities that

he helped us and maybe they'll go easy on him. I don't think he had any idea how evil his bosses are. He sure didn't look as though he was the type to take us out and shoot us in cold blood."

"Thank the Lord."

"You can say that again. We both owe God plenty. I just hope we don't have the opportunity to tell Him so in person for a few more years."

"Yeah." She scooted down in the seat and rubbed her eyes. "Are they still back there? Can you tell?"

"There's a semi between us and the Humvee but I can't imagine they'd back off after chasing us for fifty miles. I'm glad traffic is lighter on the weekends. If we were stuck in a gridlock they might get out and attack on foot and I don't want to be responsible for starting a gun battle in the middle of a busy highway."

"I'd never thought of that."

"Don't worry. We're going to get through this and then I'm going to give you the best kiss you've ever had."

"I'm looking forward to it," she said, grinning at him. "Do you really think we'll make a good couple?"

"I'm dead sure."

"Don't joke at a time like this. In case I haven't mentioned it, I'm desperately sorry for dragging you into all this."

"You're forgiven," Smith said. "Try the phone again. It looks like the truck driver behind us is going to use the Hardy bypass. If he does, we'll have closer company."

Julie Ann tried, got through to the operator, then lost the signal again. Hanging up, she said, "I am so mad at myself. I should have figured out the connection between Lester's still and the ethanol plant before I insisted we go snooping around out there. I don't understand why Denny ended up dead, though."

"Maybe he got on the wrong side of the same guy who ordered Cam to shoot us. Or maybe no one will ever know." He glanced in the rearview mirror. "Uh-oh. Our friends are gaining on us."

Julie Ann's head whipped around. She squinted as the setting sun glared off the Humvee's windshield. "Looks like there are two of them in that big old thing, like I thought." She looked to Smith and added, "For once in my life, I'm really sorry I was right."

When he said, "And for once, I agree with you," she grimaced. What had happened to her calm, peaceful life? How could everything have changed so drastically simply due to being chosen to serve on a jury? This kind of thing didn't happen to other jurors in other places, did it? Of course not. If it did, no one would ever agree to serve.

Yet she and Smith had not only stumbled into a much broader crime, they had also fallen in love—all due to jury duty. If this was merely a case of the Lord moving in mysterious ways, it was certainly one for the record books. In her wildest imagination or worst nightmare, she'd never have been able to dream up anything this bizarre. God may not have answered her prayers in the way she'd expected when she was seventeen, but He had gotten around to it eventually.

She just hoped her latest plea, the one for their mutual deliverance, wouldn't take quite so long to be answered.

* * *

Smith was sitting in the left turn lane and praying that the signal would change soon because the Humvee was now nudging his rear bumper. If they were stuck there much longer, it was possible that their pursuers would decide to climb out and he didn't want to have to run the red light in order to elude them. If he'd been alone he might have fired a shot to flatten their tires. With Julie Ann in the passenger's seat, he wasn't going to take the chance they might return fire and hit her.

"Come on, come on," he grumbled.

"They haven't moved," Julie Ann reported.

"I know. I just don't want to hang around till they have time to think of attacking on foot."

"I wonder why they haven't."

"Probably too many witnesses," Smith said flatly. He gritted his teeth and stared at the red light as if that would be enough to force it to change.

"Right. They need to be able to get away after…"

"Don't even *think* it," he ordered. "We're almost home. We're going to be okay."

Just then the signal changed and he whipped the SUV around the corner, accelerating out of the turn and racing up the hill and over the gracefully arching, four-lane bridge spanning the Spring River.

"If they didn't have four-wheel drive, we might be able to lose them by getting off the road and going cross-country," Julie Ann offered as she peered over the railing of the high bridge and looked down onto the greensward that lined the river valley for miles in both directions. "Then again, since the last flood it's probably too muddy for that."

"I don't want to chance it," Smith told her. "We're safer on the main roads and in plain sight. There's no way we're going to ditch these guys the way we did the first time. Our only real hope is if Harlan gets your messages or we make it all the way to him."

Nodding pensively, Julie Ann agreed. "I had thought, since it's Sunday night, that we might want to head for the church where there'll be a crowd. Now that I think about it, that's a terrible idea. I certainly don't want to expose anyone else to danger."

"Of course not. Going straight to Harlan's without advising him to be on guard is almost as bad. We'll just have to trust that he got the word."

Smith was hopeful as they approached, then passed, the city of Highland's police department building. Unfortunately, there was no sign of activity. If anyone was on weekend duty, they must be patrolling elsewhere.

He took a deep breath and released it with a whoosh. "Well, that's the last police station till Serenity. I'll make a quick detour past the courthouse square when we get there, just in case Harlan or Boyd are hanging around, then head for his place. The Allgoods live on Possum Trot, right?"

"Yes. And it's still early enough that Edith should be in church so we won't have to worry about anyone accidentally hurting her."

"Okay." Smith pulled into the right lane and took the corner in Ash Flat as fast as he dared, ignoring the yield

sign and speeding ahead of another semi as he nego-
tiated the turn. To his relief, the Humvee was unable to
squeeze in behind him before the big truck claimed the
right of way.

"Ha! Gotcha again," he said, casting a hopeful glance
at Julie Ann and smiling. "Luck is with us."

"Not luck, divine providence," she said soberly. "I
just hope God doesn't get tired of bailing us out before
we get there."

"He won't," Smith assured her. "I can't imagine that
He'd go to all the trouble of bringing us together the
way He has and then not follow through. You and I are
meant for each other, lady. And as soon as this is over,
I intend to show you how much."

"Is that a threat or a promise," she asked with a weak
but optimistic smile.

"A promise," Smith said. "Definitely a promise."

The SUV had passed through Glencoe and was
nearing the cement plant before Julie Ann noticed the
string of taillights that indicated a slow-moving line of
traffic ahead. She gasped and pointed. "Oh, no! Look."

"I see it. I don't dare try to pass on a curve. Even if
I managed to see oncoming headlights in time, there'd
be no way to move over enough to avoid a head-on collision. Maybe we can find a side road like you did before and slip away in the dark."

"There's no other road along here."

"You're right." Smith glanced in his mirror. "They're
still back there. They have to be."

"I know." She rolled down her window and leaned

out. "I can't tell what's going on up ahead, either. Maybe there's been an accident."

"If there has, it's possible that the sheriff is either up there already or on his way."

"Maybe it's because of us," she said, optimistic. "Maybe Harlan did get my message after all."

"Maybe. And maybe this is a trap instead of a rescue."

Her high hopes were dashed. "Do you think it could be?"

"You know as much about it as I do. It stands to reason that if we could call ahead for backup, so could the guys who've been chasing us. Get back inside and roll up that window."

"What good will that do if they decide to shoot through it?"

"Just do it. If they didn't want to start trouble in the heavy traffic in Hardy, they probably won't approach us here, either." He touched the guard's loaded pistol. "If they do, I'll be ready for them."

"Unless this whole traffic jam is their idea and we're seriously outnumbered." She trembled and laid her hand atop Smith's.

"Look, I'm sorry I suggested that. It's probably just a regular accident. Okay?" He glanced over at her. "There is something you need to know. Something I haven't felt I should tell you before."

Her fingers slipped between his and she squeezed affectionately. "Whatever it is, it isn't important. Nothing is except you and me getting out of this jam and living happily ever after."

"That's just it," Smith said solemnly. "If anything was to happen to me, I wouldn't want you to go through life not understanding."

"You love me and I love you. There's nothing else I need to understand." Julie Ann wished he'd stop insisting because she was afraid he was about to relate details of his combat experiences. When he didn't drop the subject she finally said, "Okay. But it won't matter."

"I hope not," Smith said, glancing at his mirrors and clearly remaining on alert while he spoke. "You have to believe I didn't plan this—to fall for you, I mean. I started coming to your shop for haircuts because…"

Her heart went out to him. She had never seen him struggle so hard to express himself. "You don't have to go on," she offered gently. "It's all right. Ben had trouble talking about the fighting, too."

"Fighting? No. It's not that. It's about a promise I made to Ben. He's bound to mention it eventually and I want you to hear it from me, first." Smith swallowed hard. His grip on her hand tightened. "He asked me to look after you while he was away and I said I would."

"What?" She struggled to pull free. "I'm a charity case? Again? Just like when you took me to the prom? I don't believe it. You're paying attention to me just because my stupid brother begged you to?"

"No, no. That was how it started but I fell in love with you. Maybe I always felt that way. I don't know. The only thing I'm sure of is that I'm crazy about you, Julie Ann. I want to marry you."

He finally released her hand but she didn't move away.

"Why did you lie to me?"

"I didn't. When I started to care for you I was confused. You were, too, if you'll be honest with yourself. If I had told you about my promise to Ben back then, before we were this committed, you'd have pushed me away so hard I'd never have gotten as close to you as we are now."

She had to admit he had a valid point. "Why tell me all this?"

"Because. If I—if I didn't make it—you might think I had only been pretending all along, and that would hurt far more than hearing about my agreement with Ben and knowing I really did fall for you."

"I don't know what to say."

"Don't say anything right now. Just think about it. And remember that I truly do love you, no matter what."

He was insinuating that he would give his life to save hers and she realized that she would do the same for him. Because she loved him. Clearly, Smith loved her just as much in return. It was impossible to be mad at him under those circumstances, not to mention the fact that they were still in the midst of shared jeopardy.

Up ahead, she spotted a shadowy figure motioning with a flashlight by waving it in an arc. "Look."

"I see it. He can't mean he wants me to pass all these other vehicles."

"It sure looks like he does."

"Okay. I'm going to pull out and try to squeeze by. Brace yourself and keep your seat belt on. If I have to drive off the road for safety's sake I don't want to shake you up."

"Nothing you do will shake me up any worse than

finding out my brother's the reason you paid attention to me in the first place," she admitted ruefully. "Are there any more secrets?"

"That's the one and only. I promise." He inched the SUV out of line and headed toward the man waving the light.

To Julie Ann's chagrin, a wide-set pair of lights pulled out from behind the semi at their rear and followed. She knew that Smith figured it had to be the Humvee because he was gripping the steering wheel with strong, tight fists.

"Dear Lord," she whispered, battling tears and panic. "Help us. Please."

As Smith eased his vehicle up to the man holding the flashlight, he recognized him. Logan Malloy? What in the world was *he* doing out here? He was supposed to be in church, preaching his Sunday evening sermon.

Wanting to warn the pastor, Smith rolled down his window. "That car coming up behind us is…"

"We know," Logan interrupted. "Cam phoned me and Harlan got your message a little after that, so we knew exactly which road you'd be coming in on. Just keep moving. We'll take care of everything."

"The guys in the Humvee are armed."

"We figured as much. Pull ahead and let us take over."

He gave a mock salute as he ushered them through the makeshift blockade.

Looking in his side mirrors, Smith saw the vehicle

behind them halt, as he had, only it was immediately surrounded by men brandishing rifles and shotguns.

In seconds, the occupants had gotten out with their hands raised and Harlan was cuffing them amid loud cheers and shouts from the crowd.

"Praise the Lord for country people," Smith said as he parked at the edge of the roadway. "They make a great spur-of-the-moment posse."

Julie Ann agreed. "That, they do. I'd like to go talk to Harlan. Do you think it's safe to get out?"

"You're asking me?" His grin was meant to assure her that he was teasing and he was relieved to note that she was smiling broadly in response.

"Yes, I'm asking you. Don't look so shocked. I have been known to take advice occasionally."

"In that case, I'm honored," Smith told her. He opened his door and stepped out. "Come on. It looks as if the sheriff has the situation well in hand."

Julie Ann quickly joined him and he slipped his arm around her shoulders. "I wonder where everybody came from."

"Church," one of the nearby men answered. "This is the most exciting evening service I've ever been to." He chuckled. "Brother Logan is sure going to have to go some to top this one."

Relieved, Smith accompanied Julie Ann to where the sheriff stood, speaking into his radio.

"That's right," Harlan concluded. "We got two of 'em in custody here and they're singin' like mockingbirds in May now that they know we're on to their scheme."

As soon as he signed off, Julie Ann asked, "Did they

tell you about the bootlegging operation connected with the ethanol plant? That seems to be the key to everything."

"Sure did," the sheriff answered. "There's an APB out for the brains behind the whole thing, and the Craighead County sheriff has already picked up three more who were in on it with him." He cocked his head toward the Humvee. "According to these fellas it was all about the moonshine, just like Logan figured. They had Lester and a bunch of other old boys set up to take the fall for them while they siphoned off ethanol by the truckload, sold it to a big distributor and pocketed the money."

"What about Denny?" Smith asked. "Was he in on it or was he just an innocent bystander who got in their way?"

"He was part of it, all right. Only I guess they figured he was expendable."

Julie Ann sighed. "Poor Denny. Then Lester didn't kill him after all?"

"Doesn't look like it. 'Course that'll all have to be decided in court, but it looks like Lester's going to be exonerated for everything except running a still."

Pulling her snugly to his side, Smith guided her to the side of the road so through traffic could resume as he said, "Well, I guess it really is almost over. You know what that means."

"No, what?"

"I owe you a kiss. Remember? Unless you're too mad at me to let me give you one."

She leaned closer and lifted her face to his. "Are you trying to weasel out of it?"

"No way." Smith grinned. "I will take it easy since

we have an audience. Wouldn't want to shock the church folks too much."

Giggling, Julie Ann threw her arms around his neck and stood on tiptoe to kiss him soundly.

Smith deepened the kiss, then smiled at her when their lips finally parted. "Marry me, Ms. Julie Ann Jones?"

"Are you sure that's what you want? I mean, now that the danger is past I thought you might have changed your mind."

"No way. But I will give you time to think about it," Smith told her with gentleness and understanding. "I'll wait as long as you feel is necessary. Within reason."

"I have never been known as a reasonable person," she replied. "I've been waiting for you since I was seventeen. That should be plenty long enough."

As they shared another kiss, the members of the impromptu posse cheered them on.

EPILOGUE

Although Julie Ann already knew many of the details because the jury had been officially released from duty, she was scanning the latest newspaper account a few weeks later while breakfasting with Smith at the local café.

"It says here that murder charges against Lester Taney are being dropped, thanks to the evidence Cam provided, and he's probably going to get off with probation on the other counts. So is Cam. I'm glad."

"Me too," Smith replied. "Brother Logan said there's plenty of evidence to break up the illegal distillery ring and put an end to that, too. It was a lot bigger than anyone had thought. I'm just thankful they didn't have time to kill anybody by peddling that ethanol for drinking." He put down his coffee cup and smiled across the table at his future bride. "The good guys won."

"I know. Isn't it amazing? We were right about everything." She grinned. "Well, eventually." She refolded the newspaper before laying it aside. "Maybe we should go into the private detective business. Logan could advise us and..." The look on Smith's face was so worried, she stopped. "Sorry. Only kidding."

"Good, because I know you. Once you wrap your head around something, you don't know when to quit."

"That can be a good trait," she reminded him. "After all, it means I'm not likely to change my mind about marrying you."

Smith reached for her hand and clasped it tenderly. "You still haven't told me how long you're going to make me wait."

"Not long. Becky is loaning me her wedding dress and some of the ladies in my Sunday school class have promised to decorate the church for us. All I need is for Ben to arrange a short leave so he can be here for the ceremony and we'll set a firm date."

"He's okay with all this? You told him? I wouldn't want him to show up and deck me for falling in love with his baby sister when I was only supposed to be looking out for her."

Julie Ann laughed. "Truthfully? I suspect that was what he had in mind all along. He sure didn't sound surprised to hear that we were a couple."

Smith's smile faded and he clasped her hand more tightly. "We almost weren't."

"I know. And I'll never forget our adventure, even if it did scare me to death."

"Yeah. Me too. If I'd lost you..."

Loving Smith so much, she was nearly overcome with emotion. She blinked away her tears and began to smile.

"What's so funny?"

"Me," Julie Ann said, letting her grin spread. "I was just picturing all the fun we'll have someday, telling our grandchildren the story of how we finally fell in love." She laughed. "They'll never believe it. Not in a million years."

* * * * *

Dear Reader,

Whenever I finish writing one of my books, I'm struck by the direction it has taken—no matter how it started out or what my original premise was. Many of my stories end up focusing on forgiveness, which is a universal need. This one, however, tends to lean more toward acceptance of those who are different or may seem so due to circumstances. If I have learned anything since moving to the rural Ozarks, it is that each individual is God's child and all are equally worthy, no matter what their background.

If you aren't sure of yourself in that regard, let me assure you that God loves you just as much as He loves any of His children. Are you His? It's easy to know. Just ask Him with an open heart and mind and it will be done.

I love to hear from readers. The quickest replies are by e-mail to Val@ValerieHansen.com or check out my website www.ValerieHansen.com. By regular mail you can reach me at P.O. Box 13, Glencoe, AR 72539.

Blessings,

Valerie Hansen

QUESTIONS FOR DISCUSSION

1. Have you or anyone you know ever served on a jury? How did you find the experience?

2. Who do you think make the best jurors—men or women? Why?

3. When Julie Ann is chosen to serve, she assumes that God has given her that job. Do you agree? Have you ever felt that way about a task? What was it?

4. Have you ever been to a small town like Serenity? Can you identify with the small-town flavor and customs? Would you like to live there? Why or why not?

5. Julie Ann is very feminine, yet she is comfortable handling a gun. Does that seem strange to you? Describe why.

6. When Smith finally decides to go with Julie Ann to church, do his motives seem sincere? He reveals that he accompanied other women in the past, simply to impress them. Does this bother you? Why or why not?

7. Julie Ann is independent. Do you think she was wise to hire an assistant who is so unlike her? How could this have been a good thing? A bad thing?

8. Since Julie Ann grew up in Serenity, do you think it is hard for her to be fair and unbiased in court?

9. As a result of Julie Ann's curiosity, she and Smith end up in terrible danger in the woods. She's only doing what she feels is best. Does that make it smart or right? How could she have done things better?

10. At first, the town sheriff doesn't believe Julie Ann when she tells him someone shot at her. Could it have been because he'd known her all her life? What could she have done or said to convince him sooner?

11. The town's pastor was formerly in law enforcement. Does that make him a better, more understanding counselor? How hard might it be for the congregation to accept him if he had been on the other side of the law before he turned his life around?

12. Were you surprised when townspeople came to Julie Ann and Smith's aid? Do you know others who would, too? Is that kind of caring only found in small towns or might you encounter the same loving, giving spirit anywhere?

When a tornado strikes a small Kansas town, Maya Logan sees a new, tender side of her serious boss. Could a family man be lurking beneath Greg Garrison's gruff exterior?

Turn the page for a sneak preview of their story in
HEALING THE BOSS'S HEART
by Valerie Hansen,
Book 1 in the new six-book
AFTER THE STORM *miniseries*
available beginning July 2009
from Love Inspired®.

Maya Logan had been watching the skies with growing concern and already had her car keys in hand when she jerked open the door to the office to admit her boss. He held a young boy in his arms. "Get inside. Quick!"

Gregory Garrison thrust the squirming child at her. "Here. Take him. I'm going back after his dog. He refused to come in out of the storm without Charlie."

"Don't be ridiculous." She clutched his arm and pointed. "You'll never catch him. Look." Tommy's dog had taken off running the minute the hail had started.

Debris was swirling through the air in ever-increasing amounts and the hail had begun to pile in lumpy drifts along the curb. It had flattened the flowers she'd so lovingly placed in the planters and buried their stubbly remnants under inches of white, icy crystals.

In the distance, the dog had its tail between its legs and was disappearing into the maelstrom. Unless the frightened animal responded to commands to return, there was no chance of anyone catching up to it.

Gregory took a deep breath and hollered, "Char-lie," but Maya could tell he was wasting his breath. The soggy mongrel didn't even slow.

"Take the boy and head for the basement," Gregory yelled at her. Ducking inside, he had to put his shoulder to the heavy door and use his full weight to close and latch it.

She shoved Tommy back at him. "No. I have to go get Layla."

"In this weather? Don't be an idiot."

"She's my daughter. She's only three. She'll be scared to death if I'm not there."

"She's in the preschool at the church, right? They'll take care of the kids."

"No. I'm going after her."

"Use your head. You can't help Layla if you get yourself killed." He grasped her wrist, holding tight.

Maya struggled, twisting her arm till it hurt. "Let me go. I'm going to my baby. She's all I've got."

"That's crazy! A tornado is coming. If the hail doesn't knock you out cold, the tornado's likely to bury you."

"I don't care."

"Yes, you do."

"No, I don't! Let go of me." To her amazement, he held fast. No one, especially a man, was going to treat her this way and get away with it. No one.

"Stop. Think," he shouted, staring at her as if she were deranged.

She continued to struggle, to refuse to give in to his will, his greater strength. "No. *You* think. I'm going to my little girl. That's all there is to it."

"How? Driving?" He indicated the street, which now looked distorted due to the vibrations of the front window. "It's too late. Look at those cars. Your head isn't half as hard as that metal is and it's already full of dents."

"But…"

She knew in her mind that he was right, yet her heart kept insisting she must do something. Anything. *Please, God, help me. Tell me what to do!*

Her heart was still pounding, her breath shallow and rapid, yet part of her seemed to suddenly accept that her boss was right. That couldn't be. She belonged with Layla. She was her mother.

"We're going to take shelter," Gregory ordered, giving her arm a tug. "Now."

That strong command was enough to renew Maya's resolve and wipe away the calm assurances she had so briefly embraced. She didn't go easily or quietly. Screeching, "No, no, no," she dragged her feet, stumbling along as he pulled and half dragged her toward the basement access.

Staring into the storm moments ago, she had felt as if the fury of the weather was sucking her into a bottomless black hole. Her emotions were still trapped in those murky, imaginary depths, still floundering, sinking, spinning out of control. She pictured Layla, with her silky, long dark hair and beautiful brown eyes.

"If anything happens to my daughter I'll never forgive you!" she screamed at him.

"I'll take my chances."

Maya knew without a doubt that she'd meant exactly

what she'd said. If her precious little girl was hurt she'd never forgive herself for not trying to reach her. To protect her. And she'd never forgive Gregory Garrison for preventing her from making the attempt. *Never.*

She had to blink to adjust to the dimness of the basement as he shoved her in front of him and forced her down the wooden stairs.

She gasped, coughed. The place smelled musty and sour, totally in character with the advanced age of the building. How long could that bank of brick and stone stores and offices stand against a storm like this? If these walls ever started to topple, nothing would stop their total collapse. Then it wouldn't matter whether they were outside or down here. They'd be just as dead.

That realization sapped her strength and left her almost without sensation. When her boss let go of her wrist and slipped his arm around her shoulders to guide her into a corner next to an abandoned elevator shaft, she was too emotionally numb to continue to fight him. All she could do was pray and continue to repeat, "Layla, Layla," over and over again.

"We'll wait it out here," he said. "This has to be the strongest part of the building."

Maya didn't believe a word he said.

Tommy's quiet sobbing, coupled with her soul-deep concern for her little girl, brought tears to her eyes. She blinked them back, hoping she could control her emotions enough to fool the boy into believing they were all going to come through the tornado unhurt.

As for her, she wasn't sure. Not even the tiniest bit.

All she could think about was her daughter. *Dear Lord, are You watching out for Layla? Please, please, please! Take care of my precious little girl.*

* * * * *

See the rest of Maya and Greg's story when
HEALING THE BOSS'S HEART
hits the shelves in July 2009.
And be sure to look for all six of the books in the
AFTER THE STORM series, where you can follow
the residents of High Plains, Kansas, as they rebuild
their town—and find love in the process.

REQUEST YOUR FREE BOOKS!
2 FREE RIVETING INSPIRATIONAL NOVELS
PLUS 2 FREE MYSTERY GIFTS

Love Inspired.
SUSPENSE

YES! Please send me 2 FREE Love Inspired® Suspense novels and my 2 FREE mystery gifts (gifts are worth about $10). After receiving them, if I don't wish to receive any more books, I can return the shipping statement marked "cancel". If I don't cancel, I will receive 4 brand-new novels every month and be billed just $4.24 per book in the U.S. or $4.74 per book in Canada. That's a savings of over 20% off the cover price. It's quite a bargain! Shipping and handling is just 50¢ per book.* I understand that accepting the 2 free books and gifts places me under no obligation to buy anything. I can always return a shipment and cancel at any time. Even if I never buy another book, the two free books and gifts are mine to keep forever.

123 IDN EYM2   323 IDN EYNE

Name	(PLEASE PRINT)	
Address		Apt. #
City	State/Prov.	Zip/Postal Code

Signature (if under 18, a parent or guardian must sign)

Mail to Steeple Hill Reader Service:
IN U.S.A.: P.O. Box 1867, Buffalo, NY 14240-1867
IN CANADA: P.O. Box 609, Fort Erie, Ontario L2A 5X3

Not valid to current subscribers of Love Inspired Suspense books.

Want to try two free books from another series?
Call 1-800-873-8635 or visit www.morefreebooks.com

* Terms and prices subject to change without notice. Prices do not include applicable taxes. Sales tax applicable in N.Y. Canadian residents will be charged applicable provincial taxes and GST. Offer not valid in Quebec. This offer is limited to one order per household. All orders subject to approval. Credit or debit balances in a customer's account(s) may be offset by any other outstanding balance owed by or to the customer. Please allow 4 to 6 weeks for delivery. Offer available while quantities last.

Your Privacy: Steeple Hill Books is committed to protecting your privacy. Our Privacy Policy is available online at www.SteepleHill.com or upon request from the Reader Service. From time to time we make our lists of customers available to reputable third parties who may have a product or service of interest to you. If you would prefer we not share your name and address, please check here. ☐

LISUS09

HEARTWARMING INSPIRATIONAL ROMANCE

Experience stories
centered on love and faith
with a variety of romances
just for you,
with 10 books every month!

Love Inspired®:
Enjoy four contemporary,
heartwarming romances every month.

Love Inspired® Historical:
Travel to a different time with two powerful
and engaging stories of romance, adventure
and faith every month.

Love Inspired® Suspense:
Enjoy four contemporary tales of intrigue
and romance every month.

Steeple
Hill®

*Available every month wherever books are
sold, including most bookstores, supermarkets,
drugstores and discount stores.*

Love Inspired SUSPENSE

TITLES AVAILABLE NEXT MONTH

Available July 14, 2009

WITNESS TO MURDER by Jill Elizabeth Nelson

Poised for an interview, TV reporter Hallie Berglund walks into a murder scene instead. She wants the killer brought to justice—but has she identified the right man? Her colleague Brody Jordan knows Hallie can find the truth...if she's willing to unearth the secrets of the past.

SOMEONE TO TRUST by Ginny Aiken
Carolina Justice

So what if she's the fire chief's daughter? Arson investigator Rand Mason knows too much about Catelyn Caldwell's past to trust her. Yet Cate's not the girl he remembers. And when she needs Rand's help, it's time to see if she's become someone he can believe in—and love.

DEADLY INTENT by Camy Tang

The Grant family's Sonoma spa is a place for rest and relaxation—not murder! Then Naomi Grant finds her client bleeding to death, and everything falls apart. Naomi's reputation and freedom are at stake, and her only solace is with the *other* suspect, Dr. Devon Knightley, the victim's ex-husband. But he's hiding something from Naomi....

THE KIDNAPPING OF KENZIE THORN by Liz Johnson

Myles Parsons is just another inmate in Kenzie Thorn's GED course—until he kidnaps her and reveals the truth. He's Myles Borden, FBI agent, undercover because someone wants her dead. But he promises he'll keep her safe. His heart won't accept anything else.

LISCNMBPA0609